"That's the last time I ride a horse."

Eloise wiped the last of the tears from her cheeks with her palms.

Cory led the horses toward the barn door and Eloise beelined toward the fence.

He could hear the guffaws of the ranch hands already—if he chose to tell the story, that was. They loved a good city slicker story. He wouldn't tell it, though. He knew that already. She might not be much of a cowgirl, but she didn't deserve to be mocked.

Don't fall for her, he chided himself. As she walked away, her fiery curls whipping in the wind, he led the horses into the barn.

"Lexie," he murmured to his horse. "You should have known better than to gallop with her." But it wasn't the horse's fault, nor Eloise's. It was his, for having expected something that he never should have hoped for.

Why was he doing this to himself? He had to stop this—whatever it was between them.

But right now nothing short of divine intervention would make him stop falling for her.

PATRICIA JOHNS

willfully became a starving artist after she finished her BA in English literature. It was all right, because she was single, attractive and had a family to back her up "just in case." She lived in a tiny room in the downtown core of a city, worked sundry part-time jobs to keep herself fed and wrote the first novel she would have published.

That was over ten years ago, and in the meantime, she's had another ten novels published, and her dedication to the written word hasn't diminished.

She's married, has a young son and a small bird named Frankie. She couldn't be happier.

The Rancher's City Girl

Patricia Johns

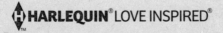
HARLEQUIN® LOVE INSPIRED®

Recycling programs
for this product may
not exist in your area.

 LOVE INSPIRED BOOKS

ISBN-13: 978-0-373-87936-6

The Rancher's City Girl

www.Harlequin.com

Printed in U.S.A.

My flesh and my heart may fail, but God is the strength of my heart and my portion forever.
—*Psalms* 73:26

To my husband, John,
who is my inspiration for all my heroes. I love you!

Chapter One

A knock on the front door echoed through the small house. Eloise Leblanc glanced quickly toward her patient. Robert Bessler lay on crisp, clean sheets, his papery eyelids closed in sleep. A fan oscillating in the corner shifted his white hair against his forehead, but he didn't stir.

Eloise pushed herself up from the chair next to his bed and stepped into the hall, angling her steps toward the front door. She paused at the door, tucking a fiery curl back into the loose bun at the base of her neck, then stood on her tiptoes to peek through the peephole. A tall man looked down, his face obscured by a cowboy hat.

Eloise paused for a moment and sucked a deep breath. *This is it.*

She opened the door and the man lifted his gaze to meet hers in frank evaluation. He pulled off his hat and held it across his chest. His hair hung in dark, disheveled waves across his forehead and his piercing dark eyes sparkled. A dusting of stubble softened his chiseled features, and he smiled hesitantly.

"Hi," he said. "Is this the home of Robert Bessler?"

"It is."

"You must be Eloise. We spoke on the phone."

"Of course. Cory?"

He nodded and she stepped back, allowing him entrance. "Your father is sleeping right now. Would you like to have a seat and wait for a few minutes?"

"Thank you."

Eloise performed a veiled inspection as Cory Stone stepped past her and into the small entryway. She'd only moved to the town of Haggerston six months earlier for the job with Mr. Bessler. She'd grown up in Billings, the largest city in Montana, and while she was well acquainted with cowboys—what Montana girl wasn't?—she still felt a sense of admiration when she saw the real thing. He loomed head and shoulders taller than she was, and his cowboy boots clunked solidly against the hardwood floor. A hint of musk lingered near, and despite his wide shoulders and obvious strength, he moved with ease.

"Please sit down." Eloise gestured into the sitting room, and the big man dwarfed the sofa as he sank into its depths.

"How is my father doing?" Cory asked.

"He doesn't have much strength left, and he's in a lot of pain," she replied, perching on the edge of a chair opposite him. "It's better to let him sleep when he's able to. Sometimes the pain keeps him awake, so the more rest he can get, the better."

Cory nodded. "It's okay. I don't want to wake him up."

"He doesn't know I called you." Eloise blushed and cleared her throat. "So this will be a little delicate."

A grin broke over the man's face. "I'll be a surprise, then."

"That's one way to put it."

"So, how did you find out about me?" he asked.

"From him."

"My father told you about me?" Cory raised his eyebrows.

Eloise paused, unsure how much information to divulge. "He always said he had no family, so when he mentioned a son, I did an online search. I was a little surprised to find you as quickly as I did. I thought it best to tell you that there wasn't much time left if you wanted to connect with him."

Cory nodded slowly and fiddled with the edge of his hat. His hands were calloused and rough, nothing like Eloise's ex-husband's smooth fingers. She swatted back the memories, irritated with how quickly they seemed to rise lately. Philip had left her for another woman two years ago. He'd moved on with the woman, but obviously, if Eloise was comparing a rugged rancher to her lawyer ex-husband, she wasn't as over him as she'd like to think.

"You didn't say how much time he has when we spoke," Cory said.

Eloise pulled her attention back to the task at hand. "I don't know. His cancer is aggressive and he's refused more treatment. So it won't be very long."

"How long have you worked for him?"

"For the past six months." Eloise glanced in the direction of Mr. Bessler's bedroom. "Your father is a very complicated man, but he has a softer side, too. I'm sure you know that."

"I don't know him at all," Cory admitted. "I've never met him."

"Never?" Eloise sucked in a breath. "You didn't think to mention that on the phone?"

"I'm sorry. I thought you knew."

"He'll be angrier than I thought." She smiled wanly and tucked that stray curl behind her ear once more. "I'd just assumed that you would have seen him at some point from the way he talked about you."

Cory looked uncomfortable. "No, ma'am. He was out of the picture before I was even born."

"I suppose I should warn you, then. The medication doesn't control the pain as well as it used to, so—"

"He's cantankerous?"

Eloise nodded. "He doesn't mince words."

"Thanks for the heads-up."

Eloise pushed the feeling of dread back down into her stomach. She'd gone through this scenario in her head a hundred times since their telephone conversation, but not once did she imagine she'd orchestrate the meeting between a son and father who had never laid eyes on each other.

This is so much worse than I thought...

A thin voice wavered from the bedroom, "Red?"

Eloise forced a smile and stood. "It looks like he's awake now. I'll be back."

As she left the room, her heart hammered in her chest. A week ago, this seemed like the best course of action, but now she wasn't so sure. Not that it mattered—the time of reckoning had come. She wished she could close her eyes and be anywhere else—a play, perhaps, or in a bustling little coffee shop in downtown Billings, a city big enough to swallow her up. Instead it was time to face the consequences of her phone call to Cory Stone.

Entering the bedroom, she found Mr. Bessler struggling to sit up, and he grunted with effort. Eloise hurried forward and helped him the rest of the way. He nodded his thanks, his breath coming in short gasps. Eloise put the breathing tubes in his nose and turned on the flow of oxygen-rich air.

"Where are my pills?" he muttered, and she pushed a paper cup of pills forward. He tipped them into his mouth with a shaky hand and slurped the water she offered him. He shut his eyes, inhaling through his nose.

"You slept for a few hours," Eloise said quietly. "How do you feel now?"

"No better. I'm dying." He opened his eyes to shoot her an irritated look.

"You aren't gone yet, Mr. Bessler." She took the cup away.

"I heard voices in the other room." He turned his head toward the wall. "You have a boyfriend visit when I sleep?"

"Hardly." She chuckled. "You give me too much credit for a personal life."

"Then who is it?" the old man demanded.

"A visitor for you."

"Who?"

Eloise turned her back to get the old man's slippers and brought them by the bed, then busied herself with his wheelchair.

"Do you want to come out to the living room to talk to him?" she asked. "Or would you rather have him come in here?"

"I'll go out there." Mr. Bessler pushed himself up and allowed Eloise to steady him as he slid his feet into the slippers. "Why on earth would I have somebody into my bedroom? Can't a man have any privacy?" He grumbled until he was settled in his chair.

"Ready now?" Eloise asked cheerily.

"Who is it?" he repeated.

"You'll see," she replied as she wheeled him out into the hallway.

"If there are balloons and a cake, you're fired," he muttered, and Eloise chuckled.

"I would expect nothing less."

As Eloise rolled Mr. Bessler's chair into the room, Cory rose. He towered over the small sitting room, broad shoulders blocking out the light from the window behind him. A piano sat against one wall, and doilies adorned every surface from side tables to the back and arms of the couch—Mr. Bessler's late wife's addition to the decor. Cory scrubbed a hand through his dark hair and he locked dark, pensive eyes on the old man.

"Whatever you're selling," Mr. Bessler said, "I'm not interested."

Cory's gaze flickered toward Eloise, then back to his father. "I'm Cory Stone."

Eloise settled her patient by the couch. She held her breath, utterly unsure of what to expect from her charge. For a long moment, no one said a word; then Mr. Bessler broke the silence.

"Your mother gave you her last name. Seems appropriate."

"She thought so," Cory agreed.

"And why are you here?" the old man queried.

"To meet you. You're my father."

"To get my estate, perhaps?" Mr. Bessler held up one finger and waggled it in his son's direction. "You think I owe you something?"

A dark look crossed Cory's face, and the muscles along his jaw tensed. "I've done well for myself. I don't need your money."

"That's good, because you aren't in my will."

Cory glanced at Eloise, eyebrows raised questioningly. Mr. Bessler scowled, and Eloise bent down close to her patient's ear.

"Mr. Bessler," Eloise murmured. "I know this is a shock, and I'm sorry about that. But this is your son."

"You're a quick one," the old man quipped.

"If you've ever wanted to speak to him, tell him something—this is your chance. You've mentioned him before, and time isn't on our side."

"It's me who has no time," he retorted. "You've got plenty."

Eloise let his comment pass, knowing from experience that he expected no reply.

The old man turned his attention to Cory. "So, what exactly do you want?"

"You're my father." Cory cleared his throat. "I wanted to—"

"Why now?" the old man interrupted. "I'm dying, you know."

Cory didn't answer.

"But you seem to know that." Mr. Bessler twisted in his chair to cast a scathing glare at Eloise, then shook his head slowly. "You called him, didn't you, Red?"

Mr. Bessler had called Eloise "Red" since her first day on the job. Lately, he'd consented to use her proper name, but the old nickname gave his words a deeper sense of betrayal.

"Yes, sir, I did," she admitted. "You've been lonely, and when you mentioned your son—" She swallowed the hot, rising anxiety. She'd crossed a line in calling her patient's son without his permission. She was here to help keep the old man comfortable. Her job did not include manipulating her patient into confrontations he wanted to avoid, no matter her intentions. While she'd truly believed that Mr. Bessler wanted to reconnect with his only son, it appeared now that she had been wrong and for one fleeting moment she wished she could go back in time and undo that phone call to Cory Stone.

"I see." The old man turned around. He nodded several times, eyeing the big man before him. "You're fired, Red," he said, his gaze pinned to his son instead of the woman he was addressing. "I won't require your services any longer."

Fired? Cory's gaze snapped between the hunched old man and his pretty nurse. Eloise blinked twice before she looked down, her long lashes veiling those deep green eyes from his scrutiny.

"Fired?" Eloise's tone registered little surprise. "Mr. Bessler, you fire me once a week. You don't really mean that, do you?"

"Why would I want a nurse who lies to me?" he barked.

"I didn't lie."

"You went behind my back," he retorted.

"Yes, sir, I did. And I'm sorry about that. It was an error in judgment. I really did think you would appreciate this last chance to know your son."

"Did you?" His voice dripped with sarcasm.

"If I'm fired, then I'll call the agency to find you another nurse." She rose to her feet and started to walk from the room, but his father heaved a sigh.

"You aren't fired," he muttered. "Come back."

She stopped, smiled and brushed a spiral curl away from her cheek. Cory didn't know her at all, but he had a good instinct when it came to character, and Eloise seemed like a good person. His father, however, hadn't exactly endeared himself yet.

Cory had expected someone more impressive. His mother had always described his father as a strong, powerful man, but this quivery gentleman looked nothing like the father he'd imagined. Frail. Old. Ornery.

I should be at the ranch, trying to find a medic to replace the guy who quit, he thought dismally. *What am I doing here? I have a hundred better things I should be doing...*

Eloise moved over to the couch and sat down. She idly adjusted a doily across the arm of the couch. The same errant curl she'd just brushed from her face fell back against her creamy skin, and Cory found his attention fixed on her. Her composure surprised him.

"So she's still your nurse?" Cory clarified.

"What is that to you?" his father asked. "I can fire her if I want to."

Eloise's gaze flicked up at Cory, and she glanced quickly between both men but didn't speak.

"Do you feel like a big man when you cast women aside?" Cory couldn't veil the chill in his tone.

"Is that your way of asking about your mother?" the

old man demanded. He coughed and slouched lower in his chair.

"No," Cory said. "My mother told me enough."

"What a horrible man I was?" his father asked with a bitter smile.

"No, she thought more of you than that."

"Where is she now?"

"She passed away a few years ago." Images of his mother's last days filled his mind. She'd died in a hospital, a gaunt figure, pain medication pumping into an IV that left a purple bruise over her bony hand. Her hair had begun to grow back in soft gray curls over her head—chemotherapy had been abandoned at that late stage of the illness. His mother had slipped away one afternoon, dying while he was out getting a breath of fresh air. He'd never fully forgiven himself for that.

His father frowned and dropped his gaze. "I'm sorry."

"Me, too," Cory said, but words could never encompass the feelings that welled up inside him when he remembered his mother's passing.

"What took her?"

"Breast cancer." Cory sat down on a chair and turned it to face his father. He hadn't decided how much he wanted to tell this virtual stranger about his time with his mother, but he had some questions of his own that he'd been waiting a lifetime to ask. He cleared his throat. "I know you don't want any kind of relationship with me, and that's fine, but I had a few things I wanted to ask you."

"Fair enough," his father replied.

"When did you meet my mother?" Cory asked.

"I don't want to talk about her."

Irritation plucked at his practiced calm. "Why not?"

He was met with a chilly silence. Eloise shifted in her seat, and Cory glanced toward her to find her green eyes full of compassion. Her pink lips parted, and he was struck anew by her unaffected beauty. Cory pulled his gaze away from her and tapped his hat against his thigh.

A smile flickered at the corners of the old man's lips. "Are you married, boy?"

Cory shook his head.

"Then I can't expect you to understand."

"Were you married when you met my mother?"

Another silence, but it seemed to answer his question.

"And you chose your wife over my mother?"

His father gave a weak shrug. "Someone had to be hurt, young man. Either your mother or my wife. I chose to protect my wife."

It explained a lot. Cory's mother had never told him much about the relationship she shared with his father, only that it was a short fling and that it hadn't lasted after she told him she was pregnant. He let his gaze move over the walls of the little sitting room, and he spotted a few faded pictures of a woman with a 1960s' hairstyle at various ages. She had a bright smile and a slim figure.

"Is that your wife?" he asked, nodding at the picture.

"Never mind Ruth," the old man snapped. "She isn't your business."

That was true, Cory knew. He wasn't even sure what to ask the old man now. He'd had a million questions over the years, but now as he faced his father, he couldn't seem to pull them out of the tangle of his emotions. One thought shot through the murky mess in his mind: *I'm the child of an affair.*

The thought had occurred to him in the past but had never been verified. Cory had preferred to believe that his mother had met a man and the relationship had simply gone sour, not that she'd been the other woman in someone else's marriage.

"I guess that's it." Cory shrugged, shoving away his

disappointment. He'd driven for two hours, at the worst possible time to leave the ranch, just to meet his father. He hadn't expected tears and hugs exactly, but he'd hoped for something—some sort of connection that would identify them as father and son. So far, he'd met with only cold disdain. "There's a lot I want to know, but you don't seem willing to talk. I'm not going to beg. Is there anything you want to know about me?"

The old man shook his head. "No."

"All right, then." Cory rose and tapped his hat against his palm. This wasn't going the way he'd expected, and while he didn't want to simply walk away from his father, he had the undeniable urge to be by himself. If he were back at the ranch, he'd get on his horse and ride, but here his options were limited. He searched the old man's lined face once more for some sign of softness but found nothing. "Thank you for your time."

Eloise sprang to her feet, but when he looked in her direction, annoyance flashed in her green eyes. She planted her hands on her slim hips and darted a look between the two men.

"That's it?" she demanded.

Both men looked at her mutely. Cory wasn't sure what she expected him to do.

"This is how you want to leave it?" She pulled the curls out of her eyes and shook her head. "Sit down."

Cory stared down at the petite woman in surprise. She raised her eyebrows at him expectantly, and he briefly considered turning his back on her, but he discarded the thought almost immediately. He sank back into his seat.

"After all these years, you can't just leave things like this."

"Sure we can," his father countered. "We've met. We've talked. We're done."

Eloise pointedly ignored the old man's retort and turned her bright gaze onto Cory. "Now, Cory, what do you do for a living?"

"I own a ranch."

"See, Mr. Bessler? That's an interesting career, isn't it?" She pulled up a chair and sat on the edge. "And what drew you to that line of work?"

"I grew up on that ranch. I inherited it."

"Does Mr. Bessler have any grandchildren?" she pressed.

"No, never married. I don't have any kids."

His father shifted uncomfortably. "What do you think you're doing?" the old man asked angrily, putting a hand on Eloise's arm.

She patted his hand. "You want to know about your son, Mr. Bessler. You're just too stubborn to admit it. You'll regret it if you just let him walk out that door."

The old man settled back into his chair glumly.

"Did you always know you wanted to work a ranch?" Eloise asked, her voice low and encouraging. She gave him an eager look, and Cory couldn't find it in himself to disappoint her. He heaved a sigh.

"Pretty much. We used to visit my grandfather on his ranch every summer. I loved the horses. I was riding before I could walk."

A smile flickered at the corners of her lips. "What about your childhood? What was it like?"

"I survived." Cory's mind went back to the years with his single mother. "We weren't rich, but my mother always found a way to stretch a penny. She was a strong woman."

"Did you miss your father?"

Cory had missed his father every day of his life. His mother had done an admirable job of raising him, but not a day went by that Cory hadn't wondered about his dad. He didn't dare mention his unquenchable curiosity with his mother, though. The few times he'd asked questions about his father, she avoided answering him, and her eyes filled with pain. No boy wanted to hurt his mother. So he wondered silently if his father ever thought about him. He didn't want to share that right now, though. Not with an old man who cared so little about his existence.

The old man heaved a guttural cough. Eloise looked in his direction for a moment, then turned her attention back to Cory. "Did you know about your father when you were young?"

"I didn't know much. My mother told me I wasn't to bother about him."

"Did you ever want to contact him?" she inquired.

Cory used to lie in bed at night as a boy, painting mental pictures of some sort of superman who would swoop into his life with a terrific excuse for his lengthy absence. He smiled sadly. "It doesn't matter."

"Fathers always matter," she replied.

The old man sat limply in his wheelchair, sunken eyes regarding him with trepidation. Cory smiled his thanks to the pretty nurse and met the old man's wary gaze.

"Did you ever think about me?" he asked.

His father was silent.

"Did you know when I was born?"

"Your mother sent me a card. At the office. You were born February twelfth."

"So you knew you had a son."

He nodded. "I knew." He licked his dry lips with a pasty tongue. "Of course I thought about you. You can't just forget something like that."

"But you never contacted me."

His father shook his head. "It was for the best."

For the best. Cory dropped his gaze. How it could possibly be in his best interest, he couldn't tell. Unless the old man was referring to his own interests.

"You didn't pay any child support, either," he pointed out. "My mother could have used the extra money."

"And you want that money now?" the old man asked.

"I'm not asking for anything from you." Cory squeezed his hat between his hands, anger rising like a salve to cover that old aching wound inside of him. "I'm the sole owner of a large chunk of property, and I can assure you that I'm not sniffing around for cash."

His father's shoulders slumped and he leaned back in his chair with a wheeze. His lids drooped. "I don't want to do this anymore. I'm tired."

The old man didn't seem to be addressing anyone in particular, but Eloise rose from her seat and bent down next to him.

"Would you like to go back to bed?" she asked quietly.

"No, I want to just sit there in the sun."

She released the locks on his wheels and eased his chair toward a pool of sunlight by a window. She bent and spoke to him in low tones. Cory stood and moved toward the door, watching the young woman as she conversed with his father. Her expression remained respectful, and after a few moments, she pulled a blanket over his knees and came back to the door where Cory waited for her.

"He doesn't have a lot of strength left," she explained softly.

"I doubt he'd have responded much differently if he were well," Cory replied.

She shrugged. "Maybe not. I'm sorry about all this."

Cory opened the front door. "Care to walk me out, ma'am?"

She chuckled at his formality.

"Mr. Bessler, I'll be back in just a moment," she said and stepped outside.

Once in the warm summer sunlight, Cory inhaled the fresh air in relief. Inside the house smelled of sickness and medicine, and as he stepped out, he longed to get back to the wide-open spaces of pasture and farmland—back to his more immediate problem of a medic who quit without notice, leaving the ranch without any medical care. He turned his attention to the petite nurse.

"Thank you," he said quietly. "You risked a lot to make that happen."

She arched her eyebrows at him quizzically. "I did?"

"Your job."

"Oh, that." Color rose in her cheeks. "Don't worry, Cory. I've still got a job. He and I have a bit of a complicated relationship, but it works."

"That's a relief." He shot her a wry grin. "I don't like to see a lady treated that way."

"He's dying." She paused, silent for a moment. "He's scared."

"You still made a conversation with him possible," he said. "I'm grateful."

"You're very welcome. Are you coming back?"

"I can't stay." His mind flooded with things he had to do. He'd driven out to Haggerston at the worst time possible.

Eloise blinked in surprise. "That's too bad. I'd hoped you two might have more time together."

"We're calving." He expected those words to suffice, but she didn't react with the knowing nod he expected.

"Oh." The look on her face told him she didn't understand.

"It's busy," he explained. "Calving is delicate— sometimes the cows need help, sometimes not." He waved it off. "Suffice it to say, I can't leave that kind of work to my partner. It's twenty-four-hour mayhem for the next little while. Not to mention, our medic quit just before I left. I have to get back."

"Oh, that makes sense." Eloise gave him an apologetic smile. "Thanks for making the trip, even for a short stay."

A short conversation didn't even begin to answer all the questions he'd been storing up, but he couldn't stay longer. Maybe if his father weren't dying he wouldn't have felt the urgency, but it was now or never.

"I...uh—" Cory cleared his throat. "I know my father probably won't agree to this, but I thought I might invite the two of you to come back with me for a couple of weeks."

"To the ranch?"

"I own about eight hundred acres in Blaine County— Milk River runs right through it. It's the best that Montana has to offer." He slapped his hat against his leg, searching for the right words. "I really want to get to know my father better, and I still have all these questions. I mean, not that I could remember them in there." He looked away for a moment, toward the ill-kept yard. "I guess what I'm trying to say is that I'd like more time with my father, but I can't stay away from the ranch any longer. If you'd come back with me, maybe that could still happen. Besides, you know him better than I do. You can get him to talk where I can't."

Cory also wanted a chance to get to know this pretty nurse a little better, but he wasn't about to say that out loud. Eloise regarded him with a thoughtful gaze.

"I feel responsible for how this turned out." She blushed. "This is all pretty much my fault, you know."

"Oh, absolutely." He shot her a wry grin. "But in the best way possible, of course."

She laughed softly. "I can ask if he'd be willing to visit—"

Cory's phone blipped and he pulled it out of his pocket

and glanced down at a text from his partner. He clenched his teeth in frustration.

"Everything okay?" she asked.

"Another injury. One of the cowboys got his arm caught in the bridle of a spooked horse. They'll have to take him to the next ranch over to get treated by their medic—"

"Does this sort of thing happen often?" Eloise asked, frowning.

"You wouldn't…" He paused, uncertain if he should even voice the idea. "Look, I know this is a bit forward, but if you and my father came to the ranch for a visit, would you consider a little extra work?"

"Replacing your medic?" she asked.

"For a couple of weeks, until we can hire someone. I'd be eternally grateful on both counts, if you're interested."

"I'll have to talk to your father and his doctor first, of course. If they agree, I'd be happy to lend a hand. You sound like you're in a bind."

He nodded. "Let me know. I'll have to head back tomorrow."

Cory dropped his hat onto his head and looked back at the house. Robert Bessler was nothing like what he'd expected, yet the chance to understand the miserable old man snagged at that boyhood longing.

Not to mention Eloise. She was beautiful, brave, confident—and the only person who actually knew his elderly father right now, and he had a feeling that her insights would be invaluable.

"I'll let you know as soon as I can," she promised and offered a smile. "It was really nice to meet you."

"Likewise." He held out his hand and took her slender hand in his. "Take care."

He gave her hand a gentle squeeze, reluctantly releasing her. She fluttered her fingers in a wave and turned back toward the door. As he trotted down the steps and strode to his pickup truck, Cory sighed.

Lord, he prayed silently, *I hope this isn't a mistake.*

Chapter Two

The rest of the day, Cory shopped for items needed at the ranch. He bought two massive bags of dry dog food, about ten packs of socks for the ranch hands and a few cases of canned food. A trip into town couldn't be wasted. By late afternoon, with errands completed, he found himself in a produce store, staring at the seasonal fruit.

He hoped that Eloise would take him up on his offer and come with his father out to the ranch. As much as he wanted time with his dad, though, his mind kept moving back to the pretty redhead. He found himself wondering about her as a woman. What did she do when she wasn't working? Did she have anyone special in her life right now? He hadn't noticed a wedding ring, but then that wasn't the surefire signal it used to be.

Cory chose several peaches from a pyramid of fragrant clingstones and dropped them into a bag. He fumbled with the bag as he tied it shut, then moved on to the next bin— plums.

Lord, this visit to see my dad didn't turn out the way I expected. I thought he'd care more, somehow. But you know him, Father. Open doors here. We don't have a lot of time.

As he headed to the counter to pay, a flash of red curls

caught his eye, and he turned in surprise. Eloise shot him a smile.

"Hi, stranger," she said. She still wore the same jeans from earlier, her embroidered top revealing the barest hint of her collarbone.

"Fancy seeing you here."

She hoisted a bag of apples. "I'm making a pie tonight after the house cools off."

"Sounds good." Cory put his purchases on the counter and nodded to hers. "My treat."

Eloise smiled shyly and she put her bag down with his while he paid. The cashier's bracelets jangled as she weighed the fruit. She gave Cory his change and he and Eloise moved toward the door together.

"The doctor gave us the go-ahead to come to your ranch," Eloise said. "If there is anything your father wants to do, this is the time to do it."

"That's great." Cory inwardly winced. That came out wrong. There didn't seem to be any right way to say things when it included someone facing death. Eloise didn't seem to notice.

"Mr. Bessler hasn't made his decision yet…" She gave him a sympathetic smile.

"I do have to head back tomorrow."

"I'll talk to him when I get back and give you a call."

"Does that mean he's alone right now?" he asked.

"No, an agency sends hospice volunteers to spend time with him. It gives me some time to myself."

The door to the grocery store shut behind them and they stepped into the glare of the afternoon sun. The scent of petunias from hanging planters mingled comfortably with the warm summer air. Shops on Main Street had kept their doors propped open and a local talk-radio show filtered out from the open door of a stationery shop, the DJ chatting away about Meagher County weather and an upcoming heat wave. Montana would serve up a hot, satisfying summer.

"I'm getting in the way of that time on your own, aren't I?" Cory tipped back his hat and grinned.

"Not at all. It's nice to have some company."

"What were you going to do with your time off?"

Eloise paused, shrugged. "I hadn't decided yet. Just go where the day takes me."

He felt a smile come to his lips. "Would you care for a walk?"

"Sure."

Cory put the bags of fruit in his truck on the way past, and they ambled up the street together. The clunk of his boots interspersed with the soft slap of her delicate sandals.

"It mustn't have been easy to hear about your parents." Eloise's voice was so quiet that he almost didn't catch her words.

"I guess there are two sides to every story," he said. "I don't know what I expected. My mother always held on to him, somehow. Wouldn't say a bad word about him. He was my father and that counted for something. To her, at least."

"He cares. He just doesn't know how to say that."

"I didn't know he was married when they—" Cory cleared his throat.

"Maybe your mother didn't know, either," she suggested.

He nodded. He hoped that was the case, at least. It was too late to ask his mother now, but the idea that she'd been involved in someone else's marriage tarnished something for him.

"His version doesn't jibe with what I was told all my life," Cory said finally. "My mother told me that my father had swept her off her feet. He was kind, knowledgeable. She said that ultimately the age difference had been too much. But that he was a good man, and she wished things had been different—for all of us."

"But she didn't want you to contact him?"

"She said it was better to give him his space. I accepted that. Looking back on it now, I can't help wondering if she wanted to avoid facing his wife. Maybe she was ashamed."

Eloise didn't answer, and she looked down, her hair, now loose in the gentle breeze, obscuring his view of her face.

"Regardless, she loved him," Cory said with a shrug.

Eloise looked up, pulling her hair back with a sweep of one hand. "You resent that, don't you?"

"What was the use?" he asked. "He didn't love her back. She spent a lifetime still caring about that man, and for what? He was married to someone else and saw her as nothing but an error in judgment."

Eloise's brow furrowed, and when the breeze shifted some curls away from her face, he thought he detected sadness in those green eyes.

"Are you okay?" he asked, his voice low.

"Fine." A smile flickered to her lips and she turned her attention in his direction.

"Liar." The smile hadn't reached her eyes.

Eloise sighed, and she didn't seem inclined to answer at first. After a moment of silence, she said, "My husband left me for his mistress."

A rush of regret hit Cory like a blow to the gut. Here he'd been, trying to untie the knot of his parents' affair, and this poor woman was the collateral damage of another affair. He winced. "I'm sorry. I'm being really callous."

"No, not at all." Eloise waved it off. "These things happen, I guess."

"No, they don't." Cory caught the bitterness in his own tone. "People don't just accidentally cheat on a spouse. It's not like a lightning strike or a tsunami."

Eloise's voice was soft. "Good point. But my situation isn't your father's, and I don't want to mix in my personal baggage."

"If it helps, I think your ex-husband must be an idiot," he said.

"It kind of does." She laughed quietly.

"So, what do you normally do on your days off?"

"I paint."

Cory raised his eyebrows in surprise. "Houses?"

"No, artistically. Pictures." She laughed and shook her head. "It's therapeutic. I've loved painting ever since I was a child, but I didn't take it very seriously until Philip left."

"Did it help you deal with all of that?" he asked.

Eloise nodded. "I realized that I'd done a lot for Philip in our marriage, and not a lot for myself. That needed to change. It's only been a couple of years, but at least I'm honoring my gifts now."

"Where's your ex-husband?"

"He has a law practice in Billings. He's remarried. They have a two-year-old daughter."

He squinted in the afternoon sunlight—the math not lost on him. "He left you for the pregnant girlfriend?"

Eloise nodded. "Afraid so. Maybe it was the right choice. At least his daughter will grow up with a father."

"And you're alone."

"Not entirely. I have God, friends, family. I'm not married, but I do have a full life."

"I didn't mean to imply—"

She shrugged. "I know, it's okay." She touched his arm, her cool fingers lingering on his wrist for a moment. "You're a good guy, Cory. I can tell."

He felt a glow of warmth at her words. He found his gaze traveling her face. Her fair complexion betrayed every passing emotion, her auburn lashes entranced him. How her husband could ever have stopped looking at her, he had no idea.

"What about you?" Eloise glanced up and he looked quickly away, not wanting to be caught staring. "What do you do on your downtime?"

"What downtime?" he joked, then grew more serious. "It's all work and no play, but I love all of it. I guess the best part is riding. Have you ridden a horse before?"

She shook her head. "I never have. Shocking for a Montana girl, I know."

"You should try it." Cory smiled. "There's no feeling like galloping across a field—pure freedom."

"One day," she agreed. "I need someone to teach me."

"I could volunteer. You'd have ample opportunity if you came out to my ranch."

"That's up to my patient at the moment."

He nodded. "Of course."

"It would be very fun, though. I could take some time to paint." She paused in her stride and looked up into his face. "I like the lines around your eyes."

"Oh?"

"Here." She raised her hand as if to touch him, then pulled back before making contact. "The lines—they speak of laughter, but also worry. And when the sun is at this angle—" She stopped, laughed uncomfortably. "I'm sorry."

"You were thinking about painting me, weren't you?"

"Just your eyes. Eyes really are the window to the soul."

They stopped as they reached another street. Beyond the intersection, houses lined the road. A little girl crouched over a driveway with a piece of chalk, and a boy sat in the grass, watching her with a bored look on his face. Somewhere in the distance, the tinkle of an ice cream truck surfed the breeze, and both children perked up immediately, then dashed toward the house, shouting for money.

"Should we head back?" Cory asked.

She nodded. "Sure."

They turned around, their pace relaxed. They moved over as a young couple walked past them down the sidewalk, hands in each other's back pockets. What was it about high school students? They seemed younger with each passing year.

"You probably know my dad better than anyone right now. I was hoping you might be able to give me some insight," Cory said.

"Maybe in time spent with him," she agreed. "But you'll know him better in other ways—the things you share."

"We don't share much," he muttered. They looked nothing alike physically—not to his eye anyway. They obviously felt differently about his mother, and their outlooks on life couldn't be more opposed. If his father hadn't confirmed that Cory was indeed his son, he might have questioned the fact.

"You share more than you think," she replied. "You're father and son. You share DNA."

"There are a lot of things I'd rather not share with him. No offense, but he's not exactly a role model to emulate."

Eloise didn't answer, but he could see in her expression that she understood. They quickly approached his truck in front of the produce store, and he felt a drop of disappointment that he had no excuse to spend more time with her. He slowed his pace.

"Do you want a ride somewhere?" he asked.

She shook her head. "No, thanks. I like the exercise."

He took the two bags of fruit from the back of his truck and handed them to her. She looked questioningly at the extra bag.

"Maybe you could give it to my dad. I thought—" He stopped, unwilling to articulate his frustration.

She held out her hand and he took it in a gentle handshake.

"I'm sure he'll appreciate it. You really are a good guy, Cory Stone."

"I'll see you," he said, then released her slender hand.

She smiled, her green eyes sparkling. "I'll give you a call when he gives me an answer."

As Eloise walked away, the bags of fruit swinging at her side and her slim, beaded sandals slapping cheerfully against the sidewalk, one thought remained uppermost in Cory's mind: as gorgeous as she was, as sweet, as interesting…

Nothing could ever develop between them. She was a tempting city girl, but a city girl nonetheless. It took a special kind of woman to fit into a ranch, and no amount of wishful thinking could change it.

Mr. Bessler sank back onto his bed. His eyes fluttered shut, then open again and he licked his dry lips. The late-afternoon sunlight glowed from behind the closed curtains, one ray of light slipping past the thick fabric and illuminating the dance of dust motes.

"How are you feeling?" Eloise asked as she counted his pills into a little paper cup.

"I need those."

"How is the pain, on a scale of one to ten?"

"Forty-two," he rasped. "I think I'm getting addicted to those pills—not that it matters at this point."

"They help with the pain, and that's what matters most."

Mr. Bessler propped himself up on an elbow to take the pills with a cup of water, then sank back onto his pillow.

"Mr. Bessler, you haven't told me yet if you want to go to your son's ranch."

"The doctor will never agree to it," he muttered.

"Actually, I talked to him and he said that now is the time to do these things."

"Forget it. I don't want to."

"Mr. Bessler, if that's your decision, then I'll support you, but I have to point something out."

He raised an eyebrow quizzically.

"If you push away Cory, who will you have left?"

"You, Red," he replied, then sighed. "That's sad, isn't it?"

"I'm great company, Mr. Bessler," she said with a wry smile. "But I'm not family."

He nodded, his eyelids drooping as the medication began to take effect. He lay silently for a couple of minutes while Eloise busied herself with tidying the small bedroom. His wife had died before him. Eloise's husband hadn't died, but his absence left a gaping hole in her life. She'd done her best to fill that gap, but she felt it. Finding someone to care about wasn't the hardest part. Trusting again after betrayal—that was the challenge, and she suspected that she and her patient had more in common than she liked to admit.

Eloise paused at Mr. Bessler's side and pressed a hand against his forehead.

"How is the pain now?" she asked. "On a scale of one to ten."

"Three."

"Much better." She adjusted a light blanket over his shoulders. "You should be able to rest now."

Eloise closed the curtains past that last ray of sunlight, dimming the room. The old man looked smaller in his bed, so frail and pale against the white sheets and blanket. Outside, children's laughter and chatter mingled with the roll of skateboard wheels. When Eloise first began working with Mr. Bessler, he'd complain about the noisy children, but he no longer mentioned them. Perhaps he'd learned to enjoy their youthful enthusiasm.

"Do you need anything else, sir?" she asked quietly.

"No…" His voice was thin and soft. From the other room, the phone rang.

Eloise looked back at her patient to find his eyes shut. She adjusted the fan so that it would reach Mr. Bessler, then slipped out the door. Eloise looked at her watch and headed toward the living room. They didn't get phone calls often. She picked it up on the fourth ring.

"Hello, Mr. Bessler's residence. This is Eloise, how may I help you?"

"Is this Robert Bessler's house?" a female voice asked.

"Yes, that's right."

"I thought he was a widower. Do I have the wrong number?"

"I'm his nurse."

"Oh, that makes sense." The woman laughed uncomfortably. "Is he there?"

"He's resting right now. Could I take a message?"

"This is Melissa Wright. I'm his cousin's daughter. We heard he wasn't doing too well."

"Who did you hear from?" she asked cautiously.

"The pastor at his church. My father used to live in Haggerston years ago. We were trying to find him to tell him about a family reunion, and the pastor told us about his situation." The woman laughed nervously. "I wish I'd gotten to know him before—before—" She cleared her throat. "Anyway, maybe I could talk to him later."

"I'll let him know that you called."

From the other room, Mr. Bessler's voice broke the stillness. "Who is that, Red?"

"Would you hold just a moment?" Eloise said, then brought the phone with her into his bedroom and covered the mouthpiece with one hand.

"This is your cousin's daughter. She wanted to say hello. Are you up for it?"

Mr. Bessler gestured for phone and she handed it over.

"Hello?" he said.

Eloise left the room to give her patient some privacy, but she could still hear his one-word responses. The quiet was truncated by grunts and "uh-huhs" coming from the other room. After a few minutes, he heaved a sigh.

"No— Melissa, was it? No. I've already written a will and decided where my estate will go."

Eloise cringed and covered her eyes with one hand.

"I understand completely," Mr. Bessler went on. "But I'm not interested in funding your education. Goodbye."

The phone beeped as he hung up the handset. For a long moment, no sound emerged from the room, but after a couple of minutes, Mr. Bessler's voice wavered as he called, "Red?"

Eloise pushed open the bedroom door. Mr. Bessler lay on his bed in the dim bedroom, the phone atop his chest. "Yes, sir?"

"That was a young woman named Melissa."

"Yes, she mentioned that." Eloise attempted to sound as impartial as possible.

"She was very thoughtful," he went on quietly. "She heard I was dying and had no children, and she very kindly offered to let me pay her school bills."

Eloise grimaced. "That's horrible."

"She'll probably make an excellent lawyer."

"I beg to differ," Eloise muttered.

"Anyhow, I told her I wasn't interested." Mr. Bessler breathed deeply through his nose. "I don't want to take any more calls from her, if you don't mind."

"Not a problem," she replied. "I'm sorry about that, sir. Some people are just heartless."

He waved it off. "It's part of the package, I'm afraid."

"What package?" Eloise asked.

"Someone has to get my money, and everyone thinks they deserve it."

Eloise remained silent, pity welling up inside her.

"The ironic thing is," the old man said softly, "There isn't much left." He laughed hoarsely.

"There might be charities willing to help pay my wages—"

"Never mind that." Mr. Bessler shook his head. "I'll pay you. But I won't let some cousin's daughter try to wring money out of my estate."

Tears misted Eloise's vision, and she blinked them back. Facing death was hard enough surrounded by family and friends. She couldn't imagine having to think about her own mortality without anyone close to her. It seemed like the time to reach out to people, but Mr. Bessler refused.

"I'm all right, Red," he said, as if reading her mind. "Don't you waste those tears on me." His eyes drooped again. "I've got Ruth up there watching over me, and the Lord hasn't left me alone yet."

"And you have me, Mr. Bessler," she reminded him.

"Maybe it's time you called me Robert," he said. "It's less formal, and you're probably the best friend I've got right now, Red."

She smiled. "Thanks. You also have a son who doesn't want anything from your estate," Eloise pointed out.

"You're right." Mr. Bessler sighed, his eyes shut. "He doesn't need it."

His breath grew even and deep, and Eloise turned to tiptoe out of the room when his voice stopped her. "Maybe I'll go see my son's ranch, after all."

Hope rose in Eloise's breast. "That would be nice, Robert."

The old man opened one eye. "I didn't say I'd be nice, just that I'd go."

Eloise smothered a grin. She was happy that the old man would have a chance to see his son, and if she was utterly truthful, she was looking forward to seeing Cory, too. He'd been more than she'd expected, somehow—gentler, more complicated, more wounded. Even now she found herself wondering about the big rancher, how he was handling all of this. Mr. Bessler shifted, seeking a more comfortable position.

"I'll let him know," she said.

"Now leave me alone," he grunted. "I want to sleep."

Chapter Three

The next morning, the house vibrated with rare excitement. Robert sat by the window, pretending not to watch for Cory's truck. He scowled at Eloise as she rechecked his oxygen tanks, but when she turned away, she'd catch the scowl fading out of the corner of her eye.

Eloise felt cheerful and upbeat about this trip. It would be good to get away from the musty little house—a holiday from the ordinary. She'd never seen a ranch before, except for what she could glean from movies, and the prospect was both exciting and mildly daunting. She had packed some painting supplies so that she could make the most of her time there.

"I'm bringing your favorite shirts—the soft ones," she told the old man as she tucked the last of the clothing into a suitcase. "I'm also packing your winter robe, just in case it gets chilly."

She chatted away to her patient, getting little response, but each time she looked over at him, she'd catch the anticipation in his eyes, quickly veiled for her benefit. When Cory's truck rumbled to a stop outside, Robert turned away from the window.

"Is he here?" Eloise asked.

"Looks like."

"Are you ready?" she asked.

"It's only a couple of hours away. You're acting like we're leaving for a month."

"I only want to be prepared." She straightened. "It'll be fun, won't it?"

He didn't answer. Instead he attempted to wheel himself toward the bookshelf.

"Can I help you with something, Robert?"

He waved her off. "I have to put something in the suitcase."

From the bookshelf, Mr. Bessler took the ornate urn that held his wife's ashes, and with some effort, he tucked it into the open bag. Eloise didn't attempt to help him. When it came to Ruth, Mr. Bessler didn't like interference.

A knock on the door drew her attention and Eloise went to open it. Cory stood on the doorstep. He pulled his hat from his head, his warm gaze meeting hers, and gave her a nod.

"Morning, ma'am."

She chuckled at his formal manners, a novelty she didn't come across often in Billings. She instantly liked it. "Come on in."

Behind her, she could hear her patient struggling to clear his throat.

"Hi, Mr. Bessler." Cory lifted his hat slightly, then dropped it back on his head and bent to pick up their bags. "Can I take these out?"

Eloise nodded and Cory's boots reverberated on the wooden floor as he headed out, his arms flexed under the weight of the luggage. She caught herself watching his muscular form as he strode back out to the truck. He was strong in a way she didn't often see. This wasn't muscle tone from working out at a gym—this was strength from hard, manual labor, and it looked different somehow, more natural. She tore her gaze away, her cheeks heating in embarrassment. Robert didn't seem to notice, much to her relief.

It didn't take long for their items to be stashed in the back of the pickup, and Eloise wheeled Robert out the side door and down the ramp. They settled the old man in the backseat of the four-door truck, his oxygen beside him. Cory then gave Eloise a hand up into the front seat before heading around to the driver's side.

"Are you comfortable, Robert?" Eloise asked.

"It'll do."

Cory hopped up into the driver's seat, the scent of his aftershave wafting through the cab. She knew he was a tall man, but proximity to him made him seem larger still. His broad hands slid over the steering wheel as he eased away from the curb, and he gave her a smile.

"I guess we'll all get to know each other a little bit," Cory said as he pulled out of the drive and into the street. "I think you'll like it out there in Blaine County, sir."

"You might as well call me Robert, too," the old man sighed. "All these formal manners are agonizing."

"Thanks. Have you always lived in town?" Cory tried again.

"All my life."

"So you must know a lot of people."

"I know them. I don't like them, but I know them."

Cory laughed. "You're direct, I'll give you that."

Mr. Bessler heaved a dry laugh.

"You said you were an accountant," Cory tried again.

"Sure was."

"You must like working with numbers then."

"I liked a steady paycheck. A married man has to provide."

"So you didn't like your job?"

"It was okay. I didn't hate it. Can't say I was passionate about taxes or anything, though."

"So what did you like?" Cory glanced into the rearview mirror. "There must have been something."

"I had a horse," the old man said quietly. "I liked the horse."

They fell into silence, and Eloise settled comfortably into the seat. They were talking, and she felt gratified. Maybe it wasn't her business, but she was glad to see the old man connecting with his son somehow.

"What kind of horse did you have?" Cory asked.

"Look, no offense, but I'm tired. Talk to her for a bit."

Cory and Eloise exchanged a look and Eloise smothered a smile. She knew her patient well enough to fully expect his bad humor, but she suspected his son wouldn't find his cantankerous nature quite so charming.

"You seem in a hurry to get back," Eloise commented.

He nodded. "Like I said before, calving is a busy time."

"What happens?"

He eyed her uncertainly. "I get the feeling that you aren't much of a country girl."

Eloise shrugged. "I grew up in Billings and moved out here for this position with your father. This is about as rural as I'm used to."

"I appreciate you coming along. You're getting me out of a bind."

"What sorts of injuries should I expect?"

"Sprains, dislocations, cuts and lacerations. Nothing we want to waste time on a hospital visit to get treated. I've got fifty-four ranch hands doing everything from cattle wrangling to maintenance and upkeep around the place."

Soft snoring rumbled from the backseat, and Eloise turned to find Robert sound asleep, his bird-like chest rising and falling.

The fields, fenced by rusty barbed wire, slipped past the window. The highway shot straight through an expanse of fields, the vast landscape dwarfed only by the sky. Huge, boiling cumulus clouds rolled overhead, their shadows slipping silently over the rolling land.

"You said you have a partner at the ranch," she said, changing the subject.

"Zack." Cory nodded. "He's a good friend. When my grandfather passed away, he left the ranch to me and two other cousins. I bought them out, and Zack and his wife, Nora, joined me in running the place. They're my management team. He's got a stake in it, of course, but the ranch is mine." He paused for a moment. "Nora is going to be overjoyed to see you."

"Because I'm a woman?"

Cory laughed, the sound deep and full. "No, because you're single and of marriageable age. She'll try to set us up, you can count on that."

Eloise felt heat in her cheeks once more. Cory's gaze lingered on her for a moment before he put his attention back on the road.

"Just don't take it personally," he said, "and we should escape unscathed."

Eloise had to admit that being set up with a handsome cowboy like Cory wasn't exactly a hardship. She stole a glance in his direction. He tapped a rhythm on the top of the steering wheel, his expression relaxed.

"And what's kept you single all these years?" Eloise asked.

Cory raised his eyebrows. He took a deep breath. "I haven't been single this whole time. I was engaged once."

Eloise eyed him curiously. She'd assumed he was the type who didn't want to be tied down. She'd come across that kind one too many times in her life, and she found herself pleasantly surprised that Cory wasn't one of that motley crew.

"What happened?"

"It didn't work out."

"Why not?" Eloise knew she was pressing, but he knew the worst about her relationship, so it only seemed fair.

"She left me at the altar."

"Ouch." Eloise winced. "Did she explain at all?"

"She left a letter back at the house. She said she couldn't live the ranch life after all. She wanted to see what the city had to offer her, and I wasn't that flexible. We wanted different things, it turned out."

Eloise nodded. She could understand that well enough. Sometimes when a couple both wanted the same thing—like a baby—and it didn't happen, the results could be equally disastrous.

Cory shrugged. "It's not that easy to handle a ranching life. My fiancée grew up on a farm, so she was no stranger to hard work."

"I guess she was no stranger to bad timing, either," Eloise muttered.

Cory laughed. "It was better that she did it before the wedding, much as that hurt."

"So what happened to her?"

He shook his head. "I don't know. I haven't heard from her since."

"When was that?"

"About five years ago."

They drove in silence for some time, the flat expanse slipping past as the miles clicked by on the odometer.

"I guess we all have our painful pasts," Eloise said quietly.

The window into Cory's past had closed. Eloise watched him surreptitiously. His dark gaze moved over the landscape, his jaw tense.

Is he thinking about the woman who left him?

She wouldn't blame him. When she was a teenager, she could eventually heal from a broken heart and move on with optimism for the future, but wedding vows had greater weight, and they took more with them when they tore free. Jesus knew what he was talking about when he said that a married couple became one flesh. They didn't separate without a lot of pain and some deep scars.

In the backseat, her patient shifted, then shifted again.

"Robert, are you all right?" Eloise asked, turning.

Mr. Bessler's eyes fluttered open. "A little sore. I'm okay."

"Scale of one to ten?"

"Fourteen."

"Cory, could we stop at the next rest area?" she asked. "It might help."

He nodded. "For sure. There's a diner coming up in about five minutes."

"Will that work?" Eloise asked.

Mr. Bessler nodded, his lips pale. "Yes. Thank you."

As Eloise took his pills out of her bag and cracked open a bottle of water, she hoped that this trip wouldn't be too much for the old man. As much as he could benefit from the new scenery, change of any kind was exhausting, especially for a terminal patient.

Cory's brow furrowed and he pressed a little more heavily on the gas pedal.

He cares.

That little fact alone eased some of her worry.

After a stop at the diner for lunch, they drove on for another hour. The truck sped over a gravel country road, dust billowing up behind them. Eloise settled back in the seat, listening to the upbeat jangle of a country tune. Cattle grazed on the swell of a hill, heads down, tails swishing. Over the foothills in the distance, a rainstorm left a gray, foggy smudge, but the sun shone brilliantly overhead where they drove.

"This is a beautiful area," Eloise said.

"This is mine." There was something in the rumble of his voice that drew her attention.

"Really?" She sat up straighter, her gaze moving over the field of green wheat out her window. "All of it?"

"Out your window is land that I lease out for crops. Out my side—" Cory jutted a thumb in the other direction "—is grazing land for my cattle. Beyond Milk River are some hunting grounds."

"Gorgeous," she breathed.

His tone was light as he said, "I might be a little biased, but I think this is the most gorgeous land in the country. There is something about the soil that keeps bringing me back home."

"You really love living out here."

"It's more than loving a location," Cory replied. "It's this ranch. Sometimes a place just becomes a part of you when you aren't looking."

Eloise didn't know how to answer, so she stayed quiet. She could sense the satisfaction in his voice when he talked about his land, his tone almost reverent. She was a city girl through and through, but cities changed constantly. New buildings went up, old buildings came down. While Billings held her memories from girlhood up to womanhood, it didn't inspire the same deep attachment that Cory seemed to feel.

The last few miles slipped by, and Cory slowed as they approached a log arch with a hanging sign that read Stone Ranch. They turned in and followed a meandering drive that led up to a sheltering copse, leaves fluttering in the constant prairie breeze. Beyond the leafy blind sprawled the house, a barn and a paddock. The house was a log ranch style, a long porch sweeping along the front with a couple of rocking chairs sitting empty. The gray barn across the way was more modern, and the paddock where several glossy horses munched hay stretched out in front of the barn. The scene reminded Eloise of pastoral paintings, all serenity in the golden afternoon sunlight. Except for that modern barn—what was it about modernity that ruined a perfectly pastoral scene?

"Zack and Nora live in the manager's house down that way," Cory said, then chuckled. "Never mind. There they are."

A man and woman emerged from the gray horse barn, both in jeans with cowboy hats pushed back on their heads. Nora wore a T-shirt with a band logo emblazoned across the front, her brown hair pulled back into a ponytail. Zack smacked a pair of leather work gloves against his thigh, a puff of dust exploding from the material. When they saw the truck, Nora raised her hand in a wave.

"Welcome back, stranger," Zack said with a grin as Cory got out of the truck.

Nora came up to Eloise's door and gave her a friendly smile and introduced herself. "You must be Eloise."

"Yes, that's me," she replied, returning the woman's infectious smile. "You certainly live in a lovely area."

"It's definitely God's country," Nora said. "Thanks for coming to help out. No injuries this morning, thankfully, but it's only a matter of time with the calving."

"Can I give you a hand?" Cory asked, poking his head back into the open window of the vehicle.

"Oh, we can handle it," Nora replied. "Zack needs to show you a weakening spot in the barn roof. I'll help Eloise get Mr. Bessler settled."

Cory raised his eyebrows at Eloise and she nodded, attempting to look more self-assured than she felt at the moment. "Go. You're needed. We'll be fine."

Cory grinned. "I'll be back soon."

As the men walked in the direction of the barn, Eloise turned to her patient.

"This is Robert Bessler."

Mr. Bessler smiled wanly in Nora's direction. "Pleasure."

"How are you feeling?" Eloise asked quietly. "How is the pain since I gave you your pills at the diner?"

"Six."

"Do you want more meds now, or after we get inside?"

"Let's get inside." He covered his mouth with the oxygen mask and took a deep breath. "And get me out of this truck. I'm nauseated."

Eloise grinned at his comforting bad humor and the two women worked together to get the old man into his wheelchair, and then pushed it toward the main house. Nora walked ahead and dropped a ramp over the stairs just before they reached them.

"This is handy," Eloise commented.

"We've been wheelchair accessible ever since Grandpa got sick. Come on in. I've got some sandwiches in the kitchen if you're hungry."

Mr. Bessler muttered something.

"What's that, handsome?" Nora asked, holding the door for them as they came into the cool foyer.

"I haven't been called that in at least a decade," he replied.

"I don't believe it." Nora chuckled. "Well, what can I feed you?"

Mr. Bessler shook his head. "Not hungry. She made me eat earlier."

"A glass of iced tea?"

The old man shrugged.

"I'll take that as a yes." A few minutes later, after Mr. Bessler had taken his medication, they sat around a pine table, a large pitcher of iced tea between them. Nora sank into the chair opposite.

"So…" Nora fixed Eloise with a cheerful smile. "Are you single?"

Eloise laughed. "Cory warned me about you."

"Did he, now? Sorry. I don't imagine you're a country girl, are you?"

Eloise shook her head. "I'm afraid not. I was born and raised in Billings and came out to Haggerston to work as a palliative care nurse."

Nora's eyebrows went up, then she glanced toward Mr. Bessler.

"Yes, I'm dying," the old man grunted. "You're allowed to talk about it."

"Well, you never know. You might find out you love all this space."

"It would be hard not to," she admitted, glancing out the window.

"Do you ride horses?" Nora asked.

"No." Eloise shook her head. "Cory mentioned teaching me how, but—"

"Take him up on that." Nora shot her a grin. "He's an excellent teacher, and there are women who would give their eye teeth for an offer like that from Cory Stone."

There was something in the other woman's enthusiasm that hinted at more than a simple riding lesson, and Eloise sipped her iced tea to avoid answering. It was flattering to be seen as a romantic option for the rugged cowboy, but Eloise wasn't exactly "on the market" again after her divorce.

The side door banged and the sound of men's voices mingled with the clomp of boots in the mudroom where the men took off their work apparel before coming into the kitchen.

"There they are." Nora stood up and headed back to the kitchen counter. "Do you two want a sandwich?" she called.

Eloise turned to see Cory amble into the kitchen.

"Robert, can I get you something else?" Cory asked.

His father shook his head. "I'm not hungry."

Cory exchanged a look with Eloise and she shook her head ever so slightly. Accepting a sandwich from Nora, Cory slipped into the chair next to Eloise.

Eloise cast about for a subject of conversation. "This is an interesting old house."

"My grandfather built it. I did some renovations when I took the place over, though."

Eloise's gaze roamed over the walnut floors, glowing from a recent polish. A rough-hewn stone fireplace dominated one side of the sitting room, the opening wide and deep, and couches surrounded it. The couches looked worn, as if they'd been used for decades, but the wear and tear only added to the charm, making her wonder about the family members who made their memories surrounding that hearth. The kitchen was large and spacious, dark cabinets combining with the walnut floors to bring a cozy feel without sacrificing space.

"A home says a lot about a person," Eloise said. "So do his friends."

"Oh no," Cory groaned. "What did she say?"

Eloise grinned. "Not too much. She's nice, though. I like her."

A smile twitched at one corner of his lips, and she chuckled.

"You seem to be the most eligible bachelor in Blaine County," Eloise offered.

"To hear Nora tell it."

"And if you tell it?"

"I don't know." He looked down at his hands. "I don't want to waste a woman's time."

Eloise knew that feeling all too well. Even though she'd known Cory only briefly, she suspected they'd understand each other perfectly. Flirting and dating might bring some excitement to her life, but she wasn't looking for compliments and a dinner out. She was past the age of playing games.

"Or your own time," she added.

"I suppose. I don't want to get involved with someone just to break up later. It's not worth the heartache."

She nodded. "I feel the same way."

"Is my dad doing okay?" he asked, lowering his voice.

The old man slumped in his chair, his eyelids drooping. Eloise put her hand over her patient's cool fingers. "Are you all right, Robert?" she asked quietly.

"Getting tired," he murmured.

"And the pain?"

"Two."

"Perfect." Eloise looked up at Nora. "Would you mind showing us Mr. Bessler's bedroom? He could use a rest."

"Oh, for sure." Nora gave her husband's hand a squeeze before heading toward the kitchen doorway. "Come right this way. I got your bedrooms ready this morning. I have Mr. Bessler in the front room—he can see the horses graze right out his window."

"Thanks for all of this, Cory," Eloise said as she rose from the table.

"It's nothing." His warm eyes met hers.

As Eloise moved around the table, she sensed his gaze following her. She felt off-kilter somehow. Staying at an attractive man's house was definitely outside her comfort zone.

The men's tones dropped as Eloise rolled Mr. Bessler from the room, and Nora chatted about the choices of bedrooms as she led the way down the hallway. She stopped in front of a door.

"I'll just let you settle in, handsome. You're next door, Eloise. Cory sleeps down the other hallway, so you'll have some privacy."

"Thank you," Eloise said. "It's really nice to meet you, Nora."

"Likewise." Nora looked back in the direction of the kitchen. "Come on back when you're ready."

Eloise rolled Mr. Bessler into his bedroom and began turning down his bed. The old man looked pale, the exertion of the trip seeming to have taken a toll.

"It's a pretty room," Eloise commented. She opened a door and peeked inside a small washroom. She shut the washroom door and surveyed the bedroom. The head of a sturdy wooden bed was in the center of one wall, a tall mahogany wardrobe looming to the side. It reminded her of the Narnia novels—the wardrobe that held the doorway to a hidden world. A wooden chair sat by the window, a folded patchwork quilt tossed over one arm. The floorboards creaked under them comfortingly, and Eloise pushed her patient closer to the window to give him the benefit of the view. The window opened up over the winding road that separated them from the horse paddock, and she paused to admire the animals. She knew next to nothing about horses, but she recognized that they were well groomed and cared for.

"You have your own private bath," Eloise said, by way of making conversation.

"That's nice."

"Nora seems friendly, doesn't she?"

Mr. Bessler didn't look inclined to cheer up. He regarded her with somber eyes. Eloise let the smile slip from her face.

"Red?" His voice wavered.

"Yes?" She squatted down next to his chair.

"I need your help with something."

"Sure. What do you need?"

"I promised Ruth I'd scatter her ashes. I never did."

"You wanted to keep her close. That's perfectly understandable."

"But I promised her." A pained look came to his lined face. "It's one more vow I've broken, and I don't like that."

Eloise nodded. "I get that. This would be a pretty place to do it."

"Lay my wife to rest on my illegitimate son's land?" He stared at her incredulously.

"What do you want to do?" she asked.

"It needs to be off this land. I can't die without doing the one thing she asked of me."

Eloise nodded. "I'll help you with that, but right now you need to rest."

Mr. Bessler let out a soft grunt as she helped him to his feet. He shuffled the few steps to the bed and sank into it with a deep sigh.

"Comfortable?" she asked.

He nodded.

"Good." She moved his wheelchair to a convenient spot out of the way. "Robert, this trip is for you and your relationship with your son. I don't want you to forget that."

"That's baloney." A smile twitched at his thin lips.

"You need to tell me if there is anything I can do to help you. That's what I'm here for."

"Oh, Red." Tenderness entered the old man's voice. "Young people are so naive. But life is shorter than you'd think. Don't waste time."

Eloise stopped short, surprised at this sudden gentleness from her short-tempered patient.

"Do you think I'm wasting time?" she asked.

"Yes," he said bluntly.

"What should I be doing differently?" she asked as she pulled the blankets over her patient.

"Living."

"I suppose we all do that in our own ways," she replied.

"No, we all stall and avoid getting close to people in our own ways," he replied drowsily. "Take a few chances, Red. When you get to my age, you don't want any regrets."

The old man shut his eyes and exhaled a slow breath. Eloise stood silently, her patient's medication sheet in her hands. Warm sunlight pooled on the floor next to the bed, and outside the window, a rabbit ventured onto the lawn, nose twitching. Was Eloise stalling? Was she avoiding?

The rabbit scampered away. With a sigh, she turned back toward the door.

Chapter Four

Cory hung up his cell phone with a sigh. A ranch hand had cut himself, and he'd need some medical attention.

"What happened?" Zack asked from where he sat at the table, putting together the work schedule for the next month.

"Barbed wire."

Zack winced. "At least we've got a medic now."

Cory nodded. "Yeah, thankfully. Can you stay here with my father while we're gone?"

"Sure." Zack shrugged. "What do I need to do?"

"We'll ask Eloise, but if he's already in bed, I doubt there will be too much."

Though Cory didn't want to disturb Eloise while she was working with his dad, he couldn't just leave a man to lose blood, either. So he headed down the hallway and knocked on his father's bedroom door.

"Yes?" Eloise opened it.

"We've got an injury. Can you come?"

"Give me two minutes. I just have to make sure your father is comfortable. Can someone keep an eye on him?"

"Zack says he can stick around. He wants to know if there is anything he needs to do."

"Just listen in case he asks for something." She flashed him a smile.

"Okay." He jutted his chin in the direction of the kitchen. "I'll be out there when you're ready."

Cory went back to the kitchen and leaned against the counter, his gaze overlooking the horse pasture. Zack hunched over the schedule, an eraser in one hand and a pencil in the other, deep in concentration.

This land—this soil—had seeped into Cory over the years. At first, it had been the summer weeks he spent with his grandfather while his mother worked in Billings in a hotel laundry room. She couldn't afford child care to watch him during school summer vacation, so she sent him to be on the ranch with her parents. This was the place he'd learned about life.

He had also learned important lessons with his mother, but times were harder in Billings. They couldn't waste money, and they carefully measured out the milk, never wasting a drop. He saw his mother exhausted from a long day at work, and he listened to those late-night conversations when she'd call her parents on the ranch and refuse to take any money.

"No, no, we're fine. I'm doing some overtime. Thanks for inviting Cory to come this summer. I'm going to miss him, though."

He'd learned thriftiness and self-reliance at home with his mother in their one-bedroom apartment, and on the ranch, he learned responsibility and hard work as he got up with the sun to start chores. He learned about delayed gratification when he raised a coop full of chicks to maturity before he started gathering eggs. He learned about the birds and the bees when he witnessed enough calves being born to spark the right questions.

His grandfather had been the male presence in his life, and those early-morning rides out to the herd when the sun eased over the horizon, or those evenings when they stood together in the mudroom, washing their hands with a big bar of soap before going in for supper, were moments that formed him.

His mother would visibly relax when she drove them up that winding drive, the worry lines in her face softening, and she'd heave a sigh of relief.

"You'll have fun this summer," she'd say. "And I'll be back in two weeks to spend a couple of days with you. You'll behave yourself, right? You do as you're told and listen to Grandma and Grandpa."

The lectures hadn't been necessary, of course. Cory wouldn't do anything to jeopardize his time on the ranch. It was the one place on earth where he could drink all the milk he wanted and roam as far as his legs would take him. Looking out over the pasture, watching the horses graze always reminded him of those summer weeks when his grandfather shouldered the pressures, and Cory got to dream about owning his own horse one day.

Who knew I'd have the ranch?

He still felt a familiar surge of gratitude at that thought. This ranch meant more to him than anything else.

A rustling sound behind him pulled him out of his memories and he turned to see Eloise in the doorway of the kitchen. She hesitated, green eyes meeting his. She pulled her curls away from her face, and her lips parted ever so slightly, and he could feel all of his orderly thoughts slipping away. What was it about this woman that addled his brain like that? He cleared his throat.

"You ready to head out?" Cory asked. "It's a pretty deep cut, apparently."

"Sure. Let me grab my supplies—"

"I've got a fully stocked kit in the truck." Cory pulled his thoughts away from dangerous territory and surveyed her attire. Her jeans were all right, but the delicate teal blouse didn't look as if it would survive long out here. Dare he say anything? There was an injured ranch hand waiting.

"Then let's go." She turned to Zack. "Thanks for checking on Mr. Bessler for me. He's almost sleeping now. His painkillers have taken effect."

"No problem," Zack said with a wave. "It's good to have you here."

She turned and followed Cory to the door, then out to the truck. He pulled open her door, then headed around to the driver's side. When he hopped up into his seat and the truck rumbled to life, Eloise eyed him tentatively. "Your father wants to scatter his wife's ashes one of these days soon."

"Okay." He put the truck into Reverse and eased out of the drive, then pushed it into Drive and headed down the gravel road. "Here?" he clarified. "Does he want me to do anything?"

It felt awkward to be suddenly so intimately aware of his father's dying wishes. Moving from boyhood fantasies of a superhero of a father to the startling reality of the dying old man was a shock to the system, and he felt mildly embarrassed at the mention of Ruth. He'd seen the pictures on the wall in the Bessler house, but so far, Ruth Bessler was little more than a shadow—a name his father mentioned with a look of annoyance shot in Cory's direction. At least right now they were a father and son in the same house, but as soon as Ruth came up, it was as if miles suddenly slid between them.

"I said I'd help him with it, so you don't need to worry." Eloise cleared her throat. "He wants to do it off your property."

Cory couldn't say he was surprised. His father jealously protected Ruth's memory, and he didn't imagine that the old man would want to lay her to rest on his illegitimate son's land.

"That's understandable," he said. He scanned the passing horse barn out of habit, his eyes skipping over each gate to check that it was locked.

"Why do you put up with him?" Cory's tone was sharper than he intended and he winced inwardly.

"It's part of the job." Eloise frowned. "But then again, he's not my father, so I don't have the same expectations you do."

"I don't have a lot of expectations. I don't even know the man."

"My patients all give me something unique. Your dad is no different."

"You must see a different side of him, because I can't get beyond his surliness."

"He definitely can be a grump. But when he talks about Ruth…he really loved her. Still does, I daresay."

Cory didn't answer. He wasn't sure how much a man could love a woman while cheating on her, and anger simmered inside him again. For all of Robert's adoration for Ruth, he hadn't been able to love his only son, and that fact still rubbed him a little raw. Eloise turned her gaze out the window and pursed her lips thoughtfully. "Is it far?" she asked.

"Just a few minutes. Things are pretty spread out around here." He cast her a grin. "Don't worry too much. This is Carl. He's tough. In fact, I had to order him to sit down and wait for us instead of going back to work with a rag tied around his hand."

She smiled. "It's different out here."

"We definitely have to be more self-reliant," he agreed.

They were silent for a couple of minutes as they bumped over the gravel road, and Cory glanced at Eloise. Her expression was conflicted, and he wondered what she was thinking about.

"Penny for your thoughts?"

Her eyes flickered in his direction, and she shrugged. "You don't want to know."

"Well, now I really do." He chuckled. "Try me."

"I was just wondering… What was the difference between your father's marriage and mine? He chose his wife. My husband chose the other woman. Why?"

Cory slowed and maneuvered around a pothole in the road. "You didn't have any suspicions about your husband?"

"I had no clue." Eloise looked pained. "I've gone over it in my head a thousand times, and I didn't see any signs. Then one day, he said, 'Eloise, I love you, but I'm not in love with you.'"

"Ouch." Cory grimaced. "That was his line?"

"That was it." Eloise rolled her eyes. "He said he'd gotten his girlfriend pregnant and he was going to live with her. He held my hand while he told me, as if I were some doddering old woman."

"Or so you wouldn't smack him."

"If that was his reasoning, it didn't work. I still smacked him." Eloise smiled, but he could see the sadness. She wasn't over it yet. "I had to start my life again while my husband shopped for cribs with his mistress."

Cory tapped the brakes as they approached a cow barn, turning into a space in front of the door.

"Marriage vows should count for more than that," Cory replied, and somehow he felt as if he should be defending the good guys out there—pointing out that all men weren't cads like her ex-husband.

"They should," Eloise agreed with a bitter sigh.

Sympathy welled up inside Cory for this petite beauty— her self-worth rocked by a man's inability to stay faithful. He didn't respect men who ran around on their wives— his father included, even though his feelings toward his father were more conflicted.

"We aren't all like that," he said, his voice low. "There are guys out there who can be faithful—who can do the right thing."

"I know." Eloise smiled apologetically. "I'm just no good at picking them."

Cory stopped the truck and pushed open the door. She followed his lead.

"Let's go find Carl," he said, hauling open the heavy barn door and gesturing her through first. Eloise narrowly missed a clod of manure and slipped into the barn ahead of him. The confiding tone between them seemed to have evaporated. It was just as well. She made him want to talk more than he should anyway.

When they arrived back at the house after treating Carl's wounded hand, Zack met Eloise at the door and headed out to the truck where Cory waited. The men had work to do, and as Cory told her, the ranch waited for no one, especially when they were shorthanded. The afternoon slipped by, Mr. Bessler woke from his nap, ate some dinner, then went to bed early for the night, exhausted by the day's travel.

The sun was hanging low in the sky when Cory arrived. His face was streaked with dust, and he greeted Eloise with a tired smile.

"Hi," she said, looking up from a cup of tea. "Wow, you look tired. Can I get you something?"

Cory smiled. "You forget that I'm a bachelor."

"Bachelors don't eat?" she joked.

"We're just prepared," he replied, chuckling. He went to the sink and washed his hands, then to the fridge and pulled out a large bowl covered in plastic wrap. He put it in the microwave and turned it on.

"You think ahead," she noticed.

"Always. That's beef stew. Have you eaten?"

"I have, actually." She smiled apologetically. "I wasn't sure when you'd get back."

Cory ran a hand through his hair and eyed her thoughtfully for a moment. "Is my dad around?"

"He's already asleep."

"Oh." He nodded. "I was hoping I might get a chance to talk to him again. I guess there is always tomorrow."

"I'm sorry about that."

He shrugged. "I've been thinking about you today."

"Oh?" Did he know how he sounded when he said these things?

"You know how we were talking about your ex-husband, and all that stuff earlier?" he asked.

Eloise nodded, eyeing him curiously. "Sure."

"Come here," he said, turning toward the doorway that led out of the kitchen. "I want to show you something."

Cory sauntered out, not even looking back to see if she was going to follow.

"This way." His deep voice reverberated through the hall, and she blinked, then walked after him.

He headed down the hallway that led away from the bedroom she'd be sleeping in that night. After they passed through the dim corridor, Cory pushed open a door at the end to a light-filled room, the last of the day's sunlight bathing it in a golden pool. Eloise stopped in the doorway, entranced by the large windows on two sides of the room, spilling long rays onto leather couches, dust motes dancing in the air. The room glowed in oranges and yellows from the tan couches to the oak floor-to-ceiling bookshelves, stocked with countless volumes. The far corner sported a small stone fireplace, swept clean. The room had the feel of a space not often used.

"What a gorgeous room," she murmured, stepping inside.

"My mother used it when she came to visit. I escape on horseback. She escaped in books."

Eloise's gaze flowed over the titles closest to her, recognizing several books by C. S. Lewis and some classic novels. The spines were old, bent, faded by the sunlight. This didn't seem like a decorative collection—these were tomes that were well loved, well read and saved for future reference.

"A girl could get lost in here for hours," Eloise whispered. Finally, on this ranch filled with land and space, livestock, rough ranch hands and a life she didn't understand, was a room that made her feel cocooned and safe.

"I had a feeling you might be a little more comfortable in here."

Cory stood in front of one of the broad windows, and when Eloise joined him, he leaned toward her, pointing along the fence line nestled in emerald-green grass to a sagging building in the distance, wind-blasted down to gray boards. The roof swooped down in a dangerous dip, one side already collapsed.

"Do you see that old barn?" he asked.

She nodded.

"When Deirdre left me at the altar, I left everyone at the church and headed straight there. I sat under that sagging roof and wondered why she didn't love me enough to stick around, try to work things out."

He turned slightly and pointed again, over the swell of a green hill. "Just over there, beyond the hill, is a copse of poplars. When I was eight and my dog died, that's where I went to cry it out. My grandfather found me about three hours later. He didn't say a word. He just dug a hole and we buried him, right there under the trees."

Cory put his hands gently on Eloise's shoulders and turned her to face the horse barn—so modern and solid compared to the dilapidated building in the field. "And that's where I had my first kiss at the age of thirteen. The girl ended up moving away with her family, and I thought

I'd never love again." He chuckled. "Young love. What can I say?"

Eloise looked up at him quizzically. She sensed that he was sharing deeply personal things with her, but she couldn't understand what point he was making.

"You have a lot of memories here," she said.

"I've got more than memories here," he replied. "I've got something big enough to hold me up. This is a place to dig down my roots and get my balance. Rain and snow can't break this land. Scorching sun can't drain it. It's bigger than me."

"Big enough to make you feel less lonely?" she asked.

"Yeah, maybe." He nodded. "It's something to rely on."

"What about God?" she asked quietly.

"Yeah, definitely. God's here, too. My faith is just as much a part of this place as my heart and my feet. When you go where God wants you, the comfort is there. Do you know what I mean?"

Eloise nodded. She'd felt God tugging her toward giving palliative care the year before, and while her work friends and family urged her to change her mind, saying she was just depressed and shouldn't add to it with a depressing job, she couldn't deny that she felt called to this job with Robert Bessler. She'd been rediscovering peace out there in Haggerston with a grumpy old man. She'd heard it said that the safest place was in the center of God's will, and she couldn't agree more.

"Deirdre didn't understand that, did she?"

"She thought I could be enough for her, but her heart wasn't in the land. At the end of the day, a person isn't enough after all."

Eloise nodded slowly. If she could have been enough for Philip through sheer effort, they'd still be married.

"What I'm getting at is, I think you need something bigger than the guy who left you. And it has to be yours—no one else's. You need some dirt under your feet, so to speak. For me, it's the land. For you—" He shrugged. "You'll find it. It's how I moved on."

"Dirt," she murmured.

"Something to remind you of who you are."

Eloise let her eyes flow over the room. She stopped at a photo on the mantel—a sun-faded color picture of a woman in her sixties with a gray streak in her hair, lines around her eyes. A pair of sunglasses was nestled on the top of her head. Her arms were crossed over her chest and her fingers, which were just visible in the frame, sported dirt under the nails.

"This is my favorite picture of my mom," Cory said.

"Why's that?"

"She was always so sad when I was a kid. But this is a picture from the year before she died. She finally found her balance."

There was something in that direct stare that dared whoever saw it to cross her. It reminded her of Cory—he'd inherited his mother's eyes. Eloise had to admit that she liked this picture, too. His mom exuded the kind of confidence that young women admired but couldn't quite obtain until they'd put in the years. The fingers, dirt under the nails, drew Eloise's gaze.

"Her hands…" She ran her finger over the glass.

"She'd been gardening. She was always gardening when she got out here."

Eloise's practiced eye moved over the hands, slightly veined, the long fingers, the unmanicured nails.

"Would you mind if I painted your mother's hands from this photo?"

Cory shrugged. "Not at all. If you want to. In fact, use this room anytime you want."

Eloise smiled her thanks, her gaze dropping back down to the portrait.

Cory glanced at a clock perched on the mantel. "I've got to eat. The stew will be done by now. Feel free to hang out here, if you want. Make yourself at home."

"I'll be just fine." She grinned.

Cory ambled toward the door. He gave her a wink; then the door banged shut behind him. Cory had a reverence for the land that she'd never encountered before. He intrigued her, but deeper than her curiosity was a certainty that while his answers were in the rich soil, hers weren't.

It won't be dirt under my nails—it'll be paint.

Chapter Five

The next morning, sunlight peeked up over the horizon and spilled down over the rolling fields toward the barn. Birds twittered softly, their song slipping in with a grass-scented breeze through the cracked window where Eloise sat in a rocking chair, her Bible on her lap.

Her prayer wasn't one with words attached, but a simple lifting of her spirit toward her Maker. She needed this time to recharge and bask in the presence of God. One of the things she liked most about being away from the bustling city was the chance to simply be still. Mornings like this one, when she had time to discern the subtle ingredients in that morning breeze—grass, dew, the softest hint of lilac—were a luxury.

Her cell phone rang and Eloise sighed, pulling herself out of the moment and reaching for her handset.

"Hello?" she said softly, keeping her voice low so as not to wake her patient next door.

"Eloise? Are you up?"

It was Cory, and she felt a smile tug at the corners of her lips. "Of course. Where are you?"

"I've been working for an hour already," he said. "Look, we have a sick ranch hand. Could you come by and take a look at him?"

"Sure." She pulled a hand through her curls and rose to her feet. "I need someone to stay with your father, though. He's still sleeping, but he'll be up soon."

"I'm sending Zack back with the truck. He can check on my dad while you drive out here."

"Where exactly are you?" Uncertainty rose inside her. Medically, she wasn't easily daunted, but she hadn't considered navigating the ranch on her own.

"Just take the main drive. It'll go past the cow barn where you gave Carl stitches yesterday, and beyond that, when there is a fork in the road, go right. The barrack is beyond. I'll meet you outside."

"Okay."

"Zack should be there any minute."

Eloise put her Bible on the bedside table and rummaged through her bag for an elastic to pull back her hair. She glanced out the window to see the pickup truck bouncing down the road toward the house.

She peeked in her patient's bedroom and he was still asleep, breathing deeply. By the time she got to the kitchen, the door in the mudroom banged open and Zack clomped inside.

"Hi," he called. "Cory said you'd be ready."

"I am." She slipped her feet into a pair of beaded sandals and held out her hand for the keys.

"You might want to wear a pair of boots," Zack said, dropping the keys into her hand. "And you drive a stick shift, right?"

It would have been wiser to admit the truth. Perhaps it was the fresh ranch air or the cautious way Zack looked at her, but she wanted to prove that she wasn't a wimp. "I'll be fine. Mr. Bessler is still asleep. When he wakes up—" she grabbed a notepad from the counter and scratched down her cell phone number "—call me here."

"Sure." Zack grinned. "Cory's waiting."

Eloise headed outside and trotted down the steps. She pulled open the heavy door and hopped up into the cab. This was a big vehicle, and she looked over the dash uncertainly. She hadn't driven a stick shift since her father taught her at the age of sixteen. She pushed in the clutch and turned the key, and the truck rumbled to life.

"Easy peasy," she said to herself, more confidence in her words than her tone, and she put the truck into Reverse and eased backward. She wasn't used to such a big vehicle, and she silently thanked God that there was nothing behind her to steer around. As she pulled onto the road, she lurched a few times when she didn't shift properly, but she was getting the hang of it as she bounced over a pothole and the rising sun slanted its beams straight into her eyes.

Eloise squinted and shaded her eyes as she passed the cow barn. A few curious cows looked up at her, chewing their cuds as they ambled out of the barn, a ranch hand behind them, slapping their hindquarters to keep them moving.

The fork in the road came up quicker than she had expected, and she slammed on the brakes, forgot to clutch and the engine died. She grumbled to herself, started it again and eased around the corner. The barrack was visible at the top of a gentle incline, and she drove the rest of the way without incident. As she eased up to the low building and parked, the front door opened and Cory stepped out.

The barrack was a low, long building with windows along the side, dormitory-style. There was no embellishment, no veranda, just brown siding and a gently sloping roof. Cory stood in the doorway, one thumb hooked in a belt loop.

"Good morning," Eloise said, hopping out. "Where is the sick man?"

"Inside." He nodded toward the building. "I forgot to ask if you drove a stick."

"I do now." She shot him a grin.

"Cute sandals."

She noted the wry tone, and Eloise eyed him curiously as he looked down at the delicate copper-and-orange beading. It was her favorite pair, pretty and feminine. "What's wrong with them?"

"Nothing. They'll last about a day and a half, though. Hope you don't mind ruining them."

Eloise smiled and shook her head. "I'm fine. What's the worst that can happen?"

Everyone seemed just a little too concerned with her footwear this morning. They really should be more concerned about that truck's transmission when she was through with it. She followed Cory inside and looked around. There were two hallways lined with doors, with one open at the end of the hallway.

Cory raised his voice to say, "Lady in the house, boys!" and the door at the end slammed shut.

"That's the shower and one of the bathrooms," Cory said. "Chad is in the room over here."

Cory knocked on a door, then opened it without waiting for response. When Eloise stepped inside, she could see why. A man lay in bed, his face ashen, a white ice-cream bucket beside him. He moaned and leaned over, spitting into the bucket. He sported a black eye and one finger was bruised and swollen.

"Oh my," Eloise murmured, moving to his side. The room was stuffy and smelled of alcohol. "Big night drinking?" she asked, putting a cool hand on the man's sweaty head.

Chad didn't answer but spat again into the bucket. Eloise looked up at Cory, but Cory's expression was impassive.

"What happened to your hand?" she asked.

Chad shook his head slowly, then stopped the motion

and moaned. "Took a swing at a guy and missed. They said I hit a wall instead."

She examined the knuckles and the swollen finger. It was broken. She bandaged his hand with the materials from the first aid kit and laid it gently across his chest.

"Other than his hand, I think it's just a hangover," Eloise said. "But people can get alcohol poisoning this way."

"Yeah, I know. I just want to make sure he's okay," Cory said.

"I'm sorry, boss," Chad said. "Won't happen again."

"Just do as the lady says," Cory replied and leaned back against the doorframe, crossing his arms over his chest. He looked annoyed, and Eloise turned back to Chad.

She took a minute to administer an antinausea medication from the medicine chest but held back on a painkiller. She knew Chad would still have a good amount of alcohol in his bloodstream, and she didn't want to mix the two.

"You're going to feel pretty miserable," Eloise told him. "Stay in bed. I want you to drink as much water as you can keep down, and I'll bring you some weak tea. That seems to help settle a stomach. You can't take a painkiller for your finger until the alcohol is out of your system."

Chad nodded, his eyes shut and his lips white. "Thanks, ma'am."

"I'll bring you the tea in a while," Cory said. "Get some rest."

Eloise rose and went to the sink to wash her hands. Before exiting the room, she heaved open the window for some fresh air.

"Do you get this often?" Eloise asked as Cory closed the door behind them.

"I don't allow drinking on my ranch," Cory replied quietly. "Once Chad is able to stand upright, I'll fire him."

Cory's voice was low but firm. Tension rippled along

his jaw line, and he glanced down at her when he noticed her scrutiny.

"I've got to have standards," he said.

Eloise nodded. "I'm not arguing."

They walked outside and Cory pulled the door shut behind him. As they walked toward the truck, a root sticking up from the ground caught Eloise's sandal. She tugged, hopping to stop her forward momentum, but it wasn't soon enough. She felt the snap as her sandal flopped away from her foot and tiny beads bounced and scattered over the gravel. Her sandal hung off her foot, one strap broken.

"Oh no..." She bent to inspect her shoe, disappointment flooding through her.

"You okay?" Cory held out a hand and Eloise slipped her fingers into his. He pulled her effortlessly to her feet, and as she rose, she found herself just inches from his broad chest. Her breath caught and she looked up into his face.

"Sorry about your sandal." His voice was quiet and low, and for a moment she imagined what it might feel like to have his arms wrapped solidly around her.

"I should have listened to Zack," she said, her voice breathless in her own ears.

"Warned you, did he?" Cory's voice stayed low and he didn't move away from her, his dark gaze moving slowly over her face.

He was so warm, so strong, so comforting standing there, that it took all of her self-control to force herself to step back. She rubbed her hands over her arms and sucked in a steadying breath.

"Let me give you a ride back." Cory gave her a grin. "I saw your driving from the window."

She laughed. "Hey, I haven't driven a stick shift since I was sixteen! I think I did pretty well!"

Cory's dark eyes glittered with humor, and he opened the passenger door. "After you, ma'am."

Gripping his hand once more, Eloise felt herself being lifted upward and into the seat. She let out a squeak of surprise, but before she could say anything, her door banged shut and Cory was walking around to the driver's side.

The ride back to the house was uneventful, and Cory dropped her off with a tip of his hat. Zack came out of the house and hopped in the passenger side and they drove toward their ranching duties, leaving her alone at the house with her patient.

"I loved these," she muttered as she took off her broken sandal. It was beyond repair, and she sadly tossed the shoes into the garbage.

After Mr. Bessler got up and had a small breakfast, Eloise suggested a walk out in the summer air, and for the first time in ages, the old man agreed. Eloise put on a pair of running shoes, making a mental note to watch where she stepped. Man-sized gum boots for a walk seemed like overkill.

The sun was high, washing out the green fields on either side of the road, bleaching the red horse barn and leaving the air warm and still. Eloise hummed as she pushed the wheelchair down the gravel road. A light blanket covered Robert's legs, despite the warmth of the day, but even her elderly patient seemed cheerier in the fresh air. Dust tickled her nose, and she found her mind wandering back to Cory in spite of her best efforts. She remembered the sensation of being lifted up into the passenger side of the truck by the strong cowboy. She sighed, pushing away the memory.

Eloise turned and looked back, the house already smaller in the distance. The cow barn loomed to the left, but she kept going forward, tugged on by that addictive horizon. At the fork in the road, Eloise turned left, away from the barrack and into what seemed to be an endless sea of waving grass, split apart by the narrow gravel road.

"Did you see my son this morning?" the old man asked.

"I did. I went to check on a ranch hand who'd had too much to drink and punched a wall."

Mr. Bessler smiled and shook his head. "Young people are idiots."

"Not all of us." She angled his chair around a pothole in the gravel road. "I'm sure you and Cory will have more time together."

Mr. Bessler shrugged his thin shoulders. "It seems a little late, doesn't it? I mean, for all this father-son bonding."

"It's never too late."

"Does he—" The old man cleared his throat. "Does he resent me?"

"You'll have to ask him," she said. "But he invited you to come here, so I think that's a good sign."

Mature trees stretched their limbs over the road, leaving dappled shade over the gravel up by the house, but out here there was nothing but sun and air. The wheelchair bumped over the rocks, and as they approached the end of the road, Eloise slowed her pace. The road tapered off, tufts of grass taking over the gravel for a few feet, and then field swallowed the rest.

"Huh," she said.

"It's hot," Mr. Bessler said. "My head hurts."

Eloise pulled a bottle of water from her bag and gave the old man a drink. A gnarled tree stood in the field a few yards off and she looked back down the road toward the house and the sheltering shade so far off.

"A bit of shade might help," she suggested.

"It would," he agreed. "Wheel me over there."

The ground was bumpy and it took all of her strength to get the chair through the tough grass and into the shade. When she got him there, she heaved a sigh of relief.

"It's a lot cooler." Eloise wiped sweat from her brow and leaned against the rough trunk of the tree.

"We have a park by our house, and it had a tree like this." He squinted up into the leafy branches. "There was a bench out there, and that's where Ruth would go when I got her good and mad. I always knew where to find her."

Eloise grinned. "You don't sugarcoat things, do you, Robert?"

"Don't see the point. Pretending things were different wouldn't change history, would it?" He arched an eyebrow.

Her patient had spent the past thirty-five years pretending he didn't have a son, but Eloise didn't see a point in bringing that up. Instead she asked, "What would you do to make her mad?"

"Oh, what do men ever do? I'd say the wrong thing. I'd criticize her mother or comment that she'd gained a few pounds. Then I'd have to go and find her. She'd be sitting out there on the bench, rain or shine. She'd be really mad the times she went out with an umbrella." He rasped out a hoarse laugh. "I'd have to apologize. She never believed me the first time, so we'd sit there together until she'd let me take her hand, and then I'd know we'd made up."

Eloise sighed. "You must have some pleasant memories with your wife, too."

"Some good, some bad. A lifetime of them make them matter more, I guess."

A crow cawed at them from the top of the tree, and farther away a swarm of sparrows wheeled and swayed through the sky as they moved from one copse to another. The field stretched before them, an ocean of green, rippling like water in the breeze.

"Do you mind if I ask you something?" Eloise asked.

"Go ahead."

"How did you do it? How did you last a lifetime with the same wife?"

"You mean, having fathered Cory?"

"No, no." The warmth of embarrassment rose in her cheeks. She didn't mean to pry into anything as personal as his affair.

"I didn't tell her."

Eloise looked at Mr. Bessler in surprise. "She didn't know?"

"Do I look crazy?" he retorted. "If telling her that her mother was a meddler and a shrew would send her out to that stupid bench, barely willing to speak to me, what do you think would have happened if I told her that I'd cheated?"

Eloise remained silent.

"I'm no fool, Red."

"They always say honesty is what makes a marriage last."

"Do they? Well, tell me this. If you could have kept your husband and never known about the other woman, wouldn't that have been better?"

Would she have preferred to stay ignorant of her husband's infidelity? Some days she would answer yes to that, but most days the answer would be no.

"Pretending things were different wouldn't change history, would it?" Eloise repeated.

Mr. Bessler waggled at finger at her and gave a faint smile.

"Cory aside," she said, "you must have had some secret that made your marriage work."

"Not getting divorced," he replied.

"Obviously." She chuckled. "But—"

"I'm serious," he interrupted. "We didn't do it. That doesn't mean we didn't fight or make each other angry. We just didn't have that option. And if I wanted a comfortable bed to sleep in that night, I'd better make her feel better, right?"

"You make it seem so simple."

"It is. You kids these days make it more complicated than it needs to be with all your books and therapists. 'Otherness.'" Mr. Bessler made air quotes with his fingers. "It's marriage, not rocket science. Your generation is a bunch of young idiots. No offense."

"None taken." Eloise laughed softly. "Maybe I'll think the same thing when I'm your age."

"Heaven help us." Mr. Bessler managed a laugh. Sheer determination hadn't been enough for her marriage, and she wondered what they'd been missing in their relationship. If she were to get married again, how could she be sure it would be different?

An image of Cory rose in her mind, and she forced it back. Why was it that every time she thought of love and marriage lately, images of Cory crowded into her mind?

"What made Ruth special, though? What made her the one for you?" Eloise asked.

Mr. Bessler shrugged. "She had me at hello the first day I met her, and she knew it."

Eloise smiled wistfully, her gaze moving out over the field and up to the sky, where a hawk slowly circled.

Ruth had Mr. Bessler's heart from the first day they met. Mr. Bessler strayed and went back to his wife. What about Eloise? Philip strayed and chose the other woman.

But I know I was a good wife.

Anger bubbled up inside her every time she remembered all that she had poured into her marriage. Eloise had been understanding and kind and seen to Philip's comfort in every way she knew how. She listened when he talked about his day. She even quit her job in order to focus on their home and reduce her stress so that they could start a family. She'd put their marriage first every step of the way. Another woman caught his eye and he walked away.

Another woman got pregnant.

If she fell in love again, what would keep her new relationship together? She missed being married and sharing her life with someone. Maybe she'd get married again one day, and was it so terrible to imagine a man in her life as handsome and rugged as Cory Stone?

"I'm ready to go back," Mr. Bessler said, rousing her from her thoughts.

"So soon?" she asked.

"I'm tired," he said. "I want to sleep."

"All right, then." Eloise braced herself and took hold of the handles of his wheelchair. With all her strength, she pulled backward. The chair lurched back, almost started moving, then sank back into the soft grass.

"Am I stuck?" Mr. Bessler's voice rose in alarm.

"Don't worry. I'll get you out."

Eloise braced herself and pulled again. The chair lifted, and instead of letting it fall back into the ruts, she tried to keep the momentum and pulled harder. Her wrist wrenched, and with a rush of pain, she had to let go. The old man grunted in surprise as the chair dropped down again.

"I'm sorry, Robert," she said through gritted teeth. "I hurt myself."

"What happened?" he demanded.

"My wrist. I think I sprained it."

"How are we supposed to get out of here?"

"I'm going to have to call Cory to help us," she said.

He eyed her archly. "I'm looking forward to you explaining your way out of this one."

Eloise stoically ignored her patient's ridicule, took out her cell phone and dialed.

Cory pulled up to a stop at the end of the road and shaded his eyes against the late-morning sun. When Eloise called saying they were stuck in a field, he'd thought she was joking and laughed. When he realized she was serious, he felt mildly guilty, hopped in the truck and drove the direction she said they'd gone.

Eloise stood under the stunted elm tree in the field, his father sitting in his wheelchair like a monarch, his head cocked ever so slightly to one side.

"What are you doing out there?" Cory called as he stepped out of the beaten-up pickup.

"Resting," Eloise called back. "We were too hot."

"Huh." A smile lifted the corners of his lips. "So you pushed a wheelchair into a fallow field?"

"At least I'm not in sandals," she retorted. "I thought it would be nice out here. Are you going to help me or not?"

Cory laughed as he picked his way across the field, his boots sinking into the soft spots. "Did you think about snakes or anthills?" he asked.

Eloise looked around them in one frantic swoop, then regained her dignity. "I think we're good."

"For now." He stopped a couple of feet from her and gave her a teasing smile.

"Cory Stone, use those big muscles of yours and get your father back to the road." She slammed her hands onto her hips. "We're hot, we're tired and your father needs to get back for a rest."

"This is true," his father piped up. "Although I am enjoying this."

"Please?" Cory prompted, then took a step back when she looked ready to swat him. "Okay, okay."

Eloise glared at him as he took hold of his father's chair and pulled it out of the softened earth. It moved easily enough, and with one heave, he pushed it to firmer ground.

"There you are," he said with a grin. "You're welcome."

Eloise gave him a sweet smile and moved behind the chair, but she favored one hand as she threw her weight behind it.

"Wait."

She glanced up, her cheeks red from heat, exertion or embarrassment, he wasn't sure which.

"What happened to your arm?"

"She hurt it," his father said helpfully.

"Let me see."

Eloise mutely allowed him to look at her swollen wrist. He slid his calloused hands over her soft arm, feeling the swell at her joint. He nodded.

"That hurt?" he asked, squeezing gently.

She sucked in a breath in response.

"I thought so." He released her arm and she cradled it against her body.

"I strained it. It'll heal."

"It'll heal better once I wrap it," he replied. "Come on. I'll push."

As the chair bumped over the grass, Cory couldn't help feeling a stab of guilt for his teasing. As ridiculous as she looked stranded in a field—what on earth had she been thinking?—he hadn't realized she'd been standing out there in pain.

"Thank you, Cory." She'd lost her fight, and in its place was a small smile. "I guess I'm used to parks, not fields."

"It's okay. I'm glad my phone was in range. It isn't always."

"I feel like an idiot."

"You should." He laughed and shook his head. "You really are a city girl, aren't you?"

Eloise gave him a wry smile. "You're enjoying this, aren't you?"

"More than I should," he admitted. "We don't get city people out here too often. Some farms are turning into dude ranches for some extra money, but I haven't gone that way yet."

"It actually sounds like a good idea."

She was naive when it came to the country, that was for sure, and the last thing he needed was anyone without a clue about ranch life wandering his property and getting stuck in a tree or worse.

"I'd spend all my time fishing tourists out of wells." He bumped his father up onto the road and grinned. "I think I'm better off sticking to cattle."

"Are they smarter?" she asked ruefully.

"They might be," he said jokingly. "They stay in herds better."

They were silent for a moment as they made their way toward the truck, and he wondered if he hadn't been a little hard on her. He'd been well aware just how green she was before he drove her out here, so he had to shoulder some of that responsibility.

"Don't worry too much," Cory said. "You have a lot to offer, and I'm glad you're here."

Eloise blushed, and he felt a wave of success at the pink rising in her creamy cheeks. She might be a city girl through and through, but she was also gorgeous—the kind of gorgeous that could make a man forget what he was supposed to be doing. And the worst part was that she seemed oblivious of her effect on him.

"Come on," he said, pushing the chair toward the truck. "Let's get you two inside."

With Eloise's directions, Cory lifted his father into the pickup truck, then boosted Eloise up beside him. She was as light as a calf, but smelled better—a combination of soap and warm vanilla. He found himself wishing he didn't have to let go, but he quickly quelled that emotion. He knew better than that.

They bumped back over the dusty road, turning at the fork, and then swooping down the mild slope toward the shade of the trees and the house. Once inside, out of the glaring sun, Eloise's fair skin looked slightly burned, but his father was none the worse for wear.

"Come on, then," Cory said. "Let's see that arm."

He rummaged around in a cupboard before he emerged with a first aid kit.

"Sit." He nodded toward a kitchen chair a few feet away from his father's wheelchair.

Her slender arm felt fragile in his big, calloused hands, and he could already see the purple bruise around the joint. She winced when he bent her wrist to see the extent of the injury.

He unwound a tensor bandage, then lifted her soft hand in his once more.

"How often do you have to bandage up your medic?" Eloise asked with a low laugh.

"You're not the first."

As Cory deftly wrapped the bandage around her arm, he could feel her relax in his hands. Slowly he wound the cloth around her wrist until her joint was properly supported. He glanced toward his father, who sat watching them with unveiled interest. He found himself suddenly uncomfortable.

"You said before that you had a horse," he said to his father to break the silence. "What kind was it?"

"An Arabian stallion."

"Nice. I have two Arabians."

The old man nodded. "They're a beautiful breed. Can they ever run."

Cory smiled—finally something in common. Arabians were bred for the desert, and they seemed to get a second wind midstride. There was no freer feeling than flying across a field on horseback.

"Where did you board your horse?"

"At a ranch just outside of town. Sometimes Ruth would come with me, but she and Soldier didn't get along."

"No?"

"He was a jealous brute."

Cory smiled. He knew the type. Horses could be territorial. He tucked in the end of the tensor bandage and turned his attention back to Eloise.

"How does that feel?"

"Better." She raised her eyes to meet his; then her gaze flickered back down to her arm. "Thank you." She pulled her hand back, examining his work. "You could be a field medic."

Cory chuckled. "I learned how to do that on calves. You'd be surprised how similar the human arm is to a cow's leg."

"I'm not sure if I should be flattered or not."

"You're better company," he offered with a grin. "And definitely smarter."

She rewarded him with a spontaneous laugh, and Cory felt happy at making her laugh. This wasn't a laughing matter, though, and he didn't think she understood exactly what could happen to her out there. That scared him. His grandfather always said that there was nothing more dangerous on a ranch than a bored city kid.

"Could I ask you a favor?" Cory said.

"Sure."

"Stay out of the fields. I don't think my insurance could take it if we didn't find you in time." He smiled, but he was far from joking. The thought of her getting hurt when his phone was out of range, or worse—he couldn't take a chance on that.

"I'm sorry about this," she said.

"I know. We don't have safety precautions set up for city folk wandering around. We work here."

She gave him a quick nod. "Understood. I'll keep to beaten paths."

"Thanks."

Cory pushed himself to his feet. "I'd better get back to work. Robert, maybe we could talk some more when I get back."

His father nodded, and Cory pulled a hand through his hair. This wasn't easy with his father watching him. He didn't know what to say, and he had a feeling that the old man could see how he felt about Eloise. He nodded in his father's direction and dropped his hat on his head.

He left Eloise sitting at the kitchen table, her gaze averted as she ran her fingers over her bandaged arm. He didn't want to see the look in her eyes. He had a feeling he'd embarrassed her in front of his father, but he didn't know how to say it any differently. If she were a man, he'd have told her off. But she certainly wasn't a man, and he wasn't entirely comfortable with the protective feeling that was rising up inside him.

Instead he had found himself flirting with the nurse— the woman who, as Nora so aptly put it, was a whole lot of pretty and not enough country. Logic had to reign.

Chapter Six

Cory hopped into the old blue Chevy pickup and turned the key. The day's work clamored for attention in his mind, but he couldn't quite forget Eloise and that strained wrist. He'd like to think he was mostly annoyed by the inconvenience, but that wouldn't be true. She'd been monopolizing his thoughts more than he liked to admit over the past couple of days.

As he crunched over the gravel road that led around the horse barn and paddock, he breathed in the sweet scent of hay in the warm afternoon sunshine.

She's not a ranching kind of woman.

If today's adventure didn't serve as a timely reminder of that fact, nothing would. But still, Eloise followed him around in his thoughts. Details like the way she glanced up at him, a smile twitching at one corner of her lips, or the scent of her perfume and shampoo mingled together—never mind that her intoxicating scent would attract every pestering insect within three yards. Even with her shortcomings, he couldn't push her out of his mind.

Not that he'd been trying all that hard, if he had to be truthful.

As Cory pulled up to the big barn, he waved at one of

the farmhands, turned off the ignition, stepped out of the truck and slammed the door shut with a bang.

"Zack is around back," the farmhand called. "One of the cows is having trouble calving."

Changing his trajectory, Cory angled around the barn and let himself through a side gate. Zack wasn't far from the open barn door, a cow in the head gate as she stamped her feet through another contraction. Zack turned when he heard Cory approaching.

"It's a hard one," he said. "She's been stuck at this stage for half an hour now. Wait, what time is it?"

"Almost two."

"An hour," Zack amended. "I was about to give her a hand. She's not going to do this one on her own."

Cory headed to the sink just inside the barn and scrubbed up before coming back to give his partner a hand. He put a hand on the cow's flank, her muscles rippling under his touch.

"Easy, girl," he murmured. "We'll help you out."

The cow huffed out her breath as another contraction came on, and Zack took hold of the calf's feet, already emerged, and gave a long, hard pull. Cory watched the cow and when her contraction ceased, he said, "Okay, stop."

Zack obeyed, and when the next contraction came, he worked with the cow's natural rhythms to move the calf steadily down the birth canal.

"I'm glad I saw her," Zack said through gritted teeth as he worked. "She tried to go off by herself. Didn't want my help."

Cory moved in to take over from his friend, grasping the calf's feet as Zack stepped back, breathing hard. He crouched down and pulled.

"I thought you'd bring that pretty redhead out with you today," Zack said.

"That pretty redhead has a name," Cory muttered, pulling steadily on the calf until he could see a nose. When the contraction ended, he stood up straight.

"Sorry. Eloise." Zack looked contrite. "Where was she?"

"In a field. Robert's wheelchair was stuck, sunk right down. She couldn't pull him back out."

"In a field?" Zack gave Cory an incredulous look. "What was she thinking?"

Cory shrugged. "No idea."

While he knew that Zack could make some hilarious jokes about city slickers being off the concrete, he found himself protective of Eloise, despite her obvious city naivete. When it came right down to it, he didn't want to make her the butt of jokes, and he didn't like the idea of anyone else laughing at her, either.

Zack patted the cow's flank. "She's bearing down."

Cory took hold of the feet and pulled again, and this time the calf's head emerged. With one final pull, the calf slid out, the birth complete. Cory bent to rub the little animal with straw, while the cow mooed softly from her restricted position in the head gate.

"I'm letting her out," Zack said, and Cory moved back to give the cow freedom to come see her calf.

Both men sat down, watching the cow lick her calf as it lifted its head for the first time, looking around.

"Eloise is a real city slicker, isn't she?"

"Seems like." Cory shook his head ruefully. "But she's here for my father. She's not here to run a ranch."

"Would be nice if she survived the week, though." Zack chuckled.

Cory shot his friend an irritated look and turned his attention back to the cows. The calf was strong, despite the long delivery, and it had already staggered up onto wobbly legs and found the mother's milk. The cow lowed softly to the calf, which was sucking noisily, milk dribbling down its neck.

"They'll be okay now," Cory said, and the men went to wash up in the barn sink.

After a thorough scrubbing, they took another look at the new calf. Some of the other cows had wandered closer to see the new addition to their herd, and Cory squinted into the sun, keeping an eye on the situation. The last thing he needed was an injured calf.

"You're interested in her," Zack said, leaning back against the fence.

Cory looked confused. "Who?"

"Eloise." Zack grinned. "And with you playing it so cool, I know I'm right."

Cory didn't answer. Instead he hooked his boot up on the fence rail in front of him and kept his eyes locked on the cow and her new baby.

"Eloise is smart," Zack went on. "Well, when she isn't getting stranded in fields. She's sweet, and she's got a great laugh. And you do talk about her a lot."

"You brought her up, not me."

"This time," Zack responded. "There's something going on there, and you know it."

"It doesn't matter."

"Of course it does," his friend retorted. "How can this not matter?"

"This ranch is my life."

"I'm still not seeing a problem," Zack replied.

"I do. Deirdre was the same."

"I've seen Deirdre rope a steer. Those two are nothing alike."

"Deep down Deirdre wanted a city life. She wanted New York and whatever they've got out there. You think Eloise is so different?"

"Have you asked her?"

"Didn't have to."

Zack chewed the side of his cheek. "I heard from Deirdre last month."

"What? You did?"

"She got married to some guy in New York."

That hit Cory like a punch in the gut. "Married, huh?"

So some other guy had gotten her down the aisle. Good to know. He clenched his teeth and turned his back on his friend.

"Do you still love her?"

Did he? Cory's competitive nature was goaded at the thought of another guy succeeding where he had failed, but that didn't constitute love.

"No," Cory said. "But it still makes me wonder what I lacked."

"A city job, I guess." Zack shrugged. "I never took her seriously when she talked about New York and all that. I mean, she was a ranch girl. I never thought you could take the country out of her."

"See?" Cory spread his hands, his point made.

"Eloise isn't Deirdre, though."

Cory sighed. "Look, it's more complicated than that. Eloise just came out of a divorce. Her husband left her for another woman."

"Left *her*?" Zack turned to give Cory an incredulous look.

"I know. The guy was obviously an idiot, but it…" He paused, looking for the words. "It blew her confidence."

"Let me get this straight." Zack wiped his hands on his jeans. "You're gun-shy from Deirdre leaving you at the altar, and she's gun-shy from that husband of hers taking off with some other woman—"

"I'm not gun-shy, I'm wiser."

Zack put his hands up. "Call it what you will."

Cory hated how well Zack could sum up his life in

twenty-five words or less. For once, he'd like to have a best friend who was equally surprised at how things turned out.

"Her husband sounds like a real piece of work. He kept things going between both women, then left his wife for the pregnant girlfriend. She never saw it coming," Cory explained.

"He did the opposite of your dad."

"Yup." His father had left the pregnant girlfriend, and his son, and chosen his wife. Was that the better choice? Probably. Although the best choice would have been to stay entirely faithful to his wife.

The cow was nursing her baby successfully, and the men turned toward the truck. They walked in silence until they got to the vehicle and opened the doors. Then Zack said, "So tell me straight: You're interested in her, right?"

"It wouldn't be smart."

"I didn't ask if it was smart. I asked if you were attracted to her."

Cory shrugged and eased into the driver's seat, slamming the door shut with an extra-hard bang. "When I settle down, it'll be with a woman who will run this ranch with me. I know what's good for me, and it's not getting all entangled with someone who wants something else."

Zack hopped into the passenger side and gave his friend a grin. "Preaching to the choir, Cory. But she's cute."

Putting the truck in gear, Cory drove toward the chores that still awaited them. Work never stopped on a ranch, and he was thankful for that. When work kept him busy, he had less time to think about the woman who waited back at the house.

Golden light from the lowering sun flooded into the library, and the shadows outside lengthened as the sky turned soft pink. The pasture looked greener in the lowering light, and the horses stood in silhouette against the sunset, silently grazing.

The side door opened and Cory's boots sounded against the floorboards in the mudroom; then the scrape of boots against a boot brush came through the walls. Eloise pulled herself from the window and listened to the direction of his movements. After a minute, his footsteps came down the hallway and there was a tap at the door.

"Come in," she called.

Cory poked his head inside. "I thought I'd find you here."

She smiled. They'd seen each other at dinnertime. Mr. Bessler and Cory had a chance to talk, and she'd made herself busy, attempting to give them some privacy. "I don't know if your father said so, but he told me that he was glad he got to talk with you earlier."

"Yeah, it was good." Cory stepped into the room. "He told me a little bit more about his accounting practice. It isn't the same as ranching, but the management part has some overlap."

"Speaking of management, how is Chad doing?" she asked. The man was legitimately ill, albeit by choice. Cory had called her that afternoon after checking on him, and he had been considerably better, but not exactly upright yet.

"He's pretty much recovered now."

"Well enough to fire?" she asked tentatively.

"He's leaving first thing in the morning. Zack has already found a replacement for him, which is a blessing, because good ranch hands aren't easy to come by."

Eloise had had no doubt that Cory would fire the man when she saw the look on Cory's face that morning. The cowboy was kind, she realized, but a man with a limit nonetheless. She wasn't sure if she'd have the guts to hire and fire that way. She'd likely feel sorry for the man and end up accepting a fraction of the work he should have been doing out of pity. Cory seemed to have the strength to face a difficult situation head-on, and he didn't seem to pity men with hangovers in the least.

"Is that hard?" she asked. "Firing someone, I mean."

"Yes and no." He shrugged. "I gave him ample warning, but it's not the fun part of the job, that's for sure." Cory's gaze fell on the small canvas she held in her hands and he moved closer, the scent of the outdoors still clinging to his clothes.

"Is this the painting of my mother's hands?" he asked.

She reluctantly handed him the canvas. It was no bigger than a book, a simple representation of his mother's hands with the dirt still under the nails. Those hands spoke volumes to Eloise, of years past, inhibitions forgotten, strength gained ever so slowly. Sometimes she wished she could skip ahead ten or fifteen years to a time when she'd have a bit more of that hard-won strength without having to endure the trials to get there. But God didn't work that way. He didn't take you over the storm, Eloise knew. He took you through it.

Cory mutely held the small canvas, and for a moment she wondered if he didn't like it or thought it trite. Perhaps it was too personal and she had overstepped by attempting it.

"Cory, I hope—"

He turned toward her, a variety of emotions showing in his rugged features.

"Can I keep it?" His tone was deep, and he raised his dark gaze to meet hers.

Eloise nodded, honored at his request. She hadn't been looking for a compliment, but Cory's wanting to have her art in his home was a more meaningful compliment than any words might be.

"You capture so much in the tiny details," he murmured.

"Those lines on her knuckles, the cuticles, that tiny break in one nail… It's like having her here, in a way."

"Hands say so much about a person." Eloise didn't know how to explain what she put into her art—that was why she painted. It represented the things she couldn't put into words.

"Why hands?" he asked.

Eloise shrugged. "It's too hard to capture a complete person—there is so much I don't know. So instead of trying to grasp all of her, I focus on one small part. Like hands. Or eyes. Maybe a pocketknife, or a wedding ring. The smaller the focus, the more I see."

A slow smile spread over his face and he nodded. "Are you hungry?"

The question caught her by surprise. Her stomach rumbled and she laughed self-consciously. "I didn't eat much at dinner."

"Come on, then."

Cory set the painting on the mantel of the fireplace next to the photo of his mother, then led the way toward the kitchen.

"How was your day?" Eloise asked.

"One of the cows had a difficult birth," Cory said, opening the fridge and pulling out ingredients. "They're both fine, though. One of the herds was spooked by some coyotes, so I put another cattle hand on duty—" He stopped and gave her a bashful grin. "Sorry, I'm rambling."

"No, go on." Eloise perched on a stool by the counter, leaning on her elbows. She found it endearing that he would think he was boring, but his life here in on the ranch was so different from anything she'd ever experienced. She found it all intriguing.

"You want to hear about this?" Cory asked doubtfully.

"Absolutely."

Cory shrugged. "Well, we have a part of fence on the

far west end of the property that needs repair. It's sagging, and one more winter will probably do it in, so I've got to put some guys on it. We have a couple of ranch hands that came with zero experience, and Chad will be gone by morning, so that will make a third new hand on staff who will need to learn the ropes around here. That means either Zack or I'll have to go do it."

As he talked, he pulled vegetables from the fridge and kicked the door shut as he pivoted and ambled back to the counter.

"Do you want some help?" Eloise asked, suddenly feeling guilty for sitting while he both entertained her and cooked.

"I'm fine." He grinned. "About time someone waited on you for a change."

Eloise felt pleased and settled back to watch him work. His hands moved nimbly with the knife as he chopped and diced.

"So, what are we having?" she asked.

"Kind of an egg scramble. Sound good?"

"Sounds great."

He pulled out a pan, then headed back to the fridge, returning with sausage. "You know, I thought I'd have more time to talk to my dad, but he sleeps a lot."

It struck her then that Cory didn't know much about the process of dying. Families were never prepared to lose a loved one, or in Cory's case, an estranged parent. How much did he feel this? she wondered. He kept a lot hidden under that tough exterior, but she knew that inside he must have been experiencing some emotions about his father.

"It's part of this stage of things," she explained gently. "The painkillers make him drowsy, but he's much more comfortable with the medication."

"Would it be…" He paused in his work. "Is he in much pain?"

"That's why I'm here." She nodded reassuringly. "I give him what he needs. There is no virtue in suffering, especially now."

Cory began to chop again, peeling the sausage's casing away from the seasoned meat.

"He's what, eighty?"

Eloise nodded. "Eighty-two."

"He would have been in his late forties when I was born."

Cory started the burner on the gas stove, the blue flame leaping up to caress the bottom of the pan. After a moment, the meat hissed against the warming oil.

Cory couldn't help that his father was dying, and in Eloise's experience, sometimes it was better to focus on other things than the impending passing of a loved one. Dying was hard, but it wasn't the biggest part of a person's life—living was. And his father was still living.

"I asked him about his marriage to Ruth today," Eloise said, attempting to move the conversation toward more cheerful ground. "I wanted to know what made it a success."

"What did he say?" Cory's dark gaze flickered up toward her, then back down to the cutting board.

"He talked about how divorce just wasn't an option. I suppose his generation was different that way."

"Hmm." Cory nodded.

"There was one thing he said that was actually rather sweet. He said that Ruth had him at hello, and she knew it."

Cory chuckled softly. "It's hard to imagine that cranky old man being romantic, isn't it?"

Eloise laughed. "A little."

Cory grabbed an onion and sliced the peel with one smooth stroke, his movements relaxing in the change of conversation.

"Did Deirdre have you at hello?" she asked.

Cory arched an eyebrow. "I don't remember. We got to know each other a little more slowly. I knew her from around town a bit, but we didn't start dating right away."

Eloise nodded.

"You want to know if there's a secret to a marriage that lasts that long, don't you?" he asked.

"Maybe I do," she admitted. "Don't you?"

"I guess. I mean, obviously I don't know what happened between my dad and his wife, but they made it to the end, at least."

Cory slid onions and peppers into the pan. Eloise was suddenly aware that she was crossing lines again. Her being at the ranch wasn't about her marriage or her personal search for answers. This was about an old man dying and his estranged son attempting to build a relationship in the last weeks he had left. A surge of guilt welled up inside of her for her fixation on herself.

"I'm really sorry," Eloise said. "I don't mean to put myself into the middle of your situation here."

"Why can't you be a part of this?" Cory caught her gaze. "You're a friend. My dad certainly sees you as more than a nurse in his life. It looks like you're pretty much all he's got."

"Thanks." Eloise wasn't sure how to answer, and she shrugged. "Things get complicated. Nursing is so personal."

Cory nodded. "Yeah, I get that. You want to know what I've been wondering about?"

"What's that?"

"Why he chose his wife over my mother. It's ridiculous, because I wouldn't have wanted my mother to break up someone else's marriage, but what made my mother the one to drop? Especially when she was pregnant with me?"

They wanted to know the same thing, apparently. She nodded.

"You must have missed having a father," she said.

"Of course. But I'm glad I listened to her and didn't look for him."

"Oh?" Eloise was surprised by that answer. She would have thought he'd resent the lost time now that his father was dying.

"Can you imagine a teenager dealing with him?" Anger flickered deep in Cory's dark eyes. "As a kid, I would have been devastated to know that my dad had no interest in knowing me."

Cory had a good point, Eloise realized sadly. Children needed love and encouragement, and his father hadn't been able to provide those things.

"It sounds like you had a good mom, though," she offered.

"I did." The fork ticked lightly against the side of the bowl as he whisked the eggs. "I had a good life. From this side of things, I have to say that I was better off with my fantasies than I was knowing the truth about my father."

Someone had to get hurt. Wasn't that what the old man had said? One stupid decision, and someone's life would be ruined—he just had to pick the woman to cast aside.

Yet, against all odds, he'd chosen his wife, and in a strange way that comforted Eloise. Even in grouchy old Mr. Bessler, there was something stronger than his attraction to a younger woman—something that kept him with the woman to whom he'd made vows.

"I think he missed out in not knowing you," Eloise said. "I have a feeling he would have been a different man if he'd taken the risk to reach out to you."

Cory shrugged. "Maybe not. Who knows if Ruth even knew about me."

Eloise sighed. *Someone had to get hurt.* Just not Robert Bessler.

Cory poured the eggs over the vegetables and sausage in the pan, and the mixture sizzled deliciously.

Eloise looked around the warmly lit kitchen. Robert was another subject she'd never be able to fully comprehend. He was a perplexing old man, and no matter how hard she tried to make sense of his motives, she came up short.

"I don't know what makes for a lasting marriage," Cory admitted as he spooned steaming eggs, vegetables and sausage from the pan onto plates. "When I do find the right woman and get married, I'm not going to make my father's mistakes."

Eloise nodded. "You're different from him."

Cory pushed a fork across the counter, then placed a plate in front of her. "Eat up. Out in the country, we don't count calories. We burn them off."

Eloise laughed out loud and picked up the fork.

Chapter Seven

Afternoon sunlight spilled down the hallway from the dining-room window, warming Eloise's legs as she pushed open Mr. Bessler's bedroom door and peeked inside. He lay in the dimmed room, his chest rising and falling with each soft snore. She eased the door shut again with a click and stood with her hand on the knob. The morning had been busy. A ranch hand dislocated his shoulder in a riding accident, and then another man had broken a toe when a heifer stepped on it. Zack had driven her from patient to patient, and Nora had volunteered to stay with Mr. Bessler as he slept.

Now that Eloise was back again, she'd been planning on taking the old man into town so she could get a few items from the drugstore and give him some different scenery. She thought he might enjoy it, but today he was more exhausted than usual. The last stretch for a terminal patient was the hardest on everyone, especially the patient.

"Eloise?"

Cory ambled down the hallway, then stopped short when he saw her face. "Is he okay?"

"He's still sleeping. I checked his vital signs earlier, and he's doing well, considering."

He nodded. "You look worried."

"I'd hoped to get into town today and buy him a few supplies. You could also use some more antinausea medication. I used up the last of your stock for Chad."

"Good point." Cory nodded. "I can give you a ride if you like."

"But your father is still sleeping." Days like this were difficult for a nurse. Mr. Bessler had slept most of the morning, woken for a few hours around noon, and had just fallen back asleep. Her patient needed someone with him, but beyond that, the hours crawled by.

"Follow me." Cory headed back toward the kitchen and Eloise followed.

Nora looked up from the table, which was covered in ledgers. A pencil was balanced behind her ear and she clutched a pen in one hand. She bent over the books and ran a hand through her straight, shoulder-length hair. "Sorry to eavesdrop, but I'm going to be here all afternoon if you'd like me to keep an eye on Mr. Bessler. We're redoing the kitchen floor over at our place, so it's kind of a mess over there."

Cory raised his eyebrows questioningly and Eloise pressed her lips together, considering for a moment.

"You've already done that once today," Eloise replied. "I don't want to impose."

"I'm here anyway," Nora replied with a shrug. "It doesn't put me out."

"If you could just look in on him once every twenty minutes or so. He's sleeping normally right now. He's already had his pain medication and shouldn't have more until I return. If anything changes—if he complains about pain, seems short of breath, or anything like that—you could call me on my cell phone."

Nora nodded. "Definitely."

Eloise smiled. "Thanks, Nora, I really appreciate it."

"No problem." Nora shot Eloise a smile. "You could use some time off, you know."

Eloise shrugged. Nursing didn't offer regular breaks—her focus was the patient. That being said, she was starting to tire out.

"A trip to town takes an hour if we rush, a couple of hours if we stop for coffee." Cory picked up an apple from the fruit bowl on the counter and polished it against his shirt. "We don't have to be gone too long."

"A couple of hours is just fine." Nora dropped her gaze to her ledgers and waved Cory and Eloise away. "Have fun."

Ten minutes later, Cory and Eloise bumped along the drive toward the highway in Cory's black pickup. Eloise leaned her head back, feeling the tension slide out of her neck and shoulders. Cranton was a twenty-minute drive from the ranch, a drive interspersed with billowing dust from gravel roads and the melancholy jangle from the radio. After a short drive on the main highway, another lengthy road led them into Cranton, a farming community nestled in the middle of rolling fields on all four sides, swallowed up in crops. The town consisted of a couple of small schools, a grocery store and a few streets of storefronts and local businesses, thrown together with rare abandon. The seed store hunched right next door to the local burger joint, and the mayor's office was next to a butcher on one side, and what appeared to be a closed auto body shop on the other.

"This is 'town'?" Eloise asked, looking out the window. A leather and tackle shop looked all but closed, except that the door was propped open with a brick and an old man sat in front, his chair tipped back against the brick wall behind him. Cory beeped his horn and the old man raised his hat, then dropped it back over his eyes in response.

"This is Cranton, in all its glory."

"And I thought Haggerston was little," she murmured.

"We make do," Cory replied, nonplussed.

"Isn't it lonely out here, so far from everything?"

"Lonely?" Cory laughed. "You really aren't used to small towns, are you?"

Eloise wasn't sure what he meant, but the place looked downright dead. A few stores were open, a handful of pickup trucks left clouds of dust behind them as they rumbled through town, but other than the man sitting outside the leather shop, she couldn't see any signs of life. If Haggerston, where Mr. Bessler lived, was a small town, Cranton was microscopic.

Eloise's errands didn't take long. The drugstore, sandwiched between the hardware store and general fix-it shop, was surprisingly well stocked, and she was able to get everything she needed in a matter of minutes. Waiting for the owner of the store to stop chatting with an older lady and ring up her order, however, took a full fifteen minutes. All included, before half an hour passed, Cory and Eloise pulled into the only establishment that seemed to have any customers: Liza's Diner.

"The coffee is hot and the pie is amazing," Cory said. "It'll do you good."

Liza's Diner crouched long and low, just outside Cranton on the gravel road that led back to the highway. A red-and-white-striped awning shaded the front door. An Open sign flickered in the window, and next to it, a faded Montana Beef loyalty sign showed a brown cow, staring at the camera, a tuft of grass hanging out one side of its mouth.

Cory opened the door and Eloise stepped into the stuffy dining room. It didn't look as if it had been updated since the day it opened, sometime in the seventies it appeared. Brown wooden tables were scattered over an orangey carpet, white-and-red-checkered cloths covered half of the tables, while the rest were bare. The patrons of the diner were obviously local folk from farms and ranches in the area. Two waitresses worked the room with a pot of coffee in each hand. Voices mingled with the clatter of cooking that emanated from behind a swinging door that heaved open every couple of minutes, a server emerging with a tray of steaming food.

"Hey, Cory Stone." An old rancher grinned up from a plate of steak and eggs. "How's the calving, son?"

"Steady. How about you, Earl?"

"Lost two calves last night. Twins."

"Sorry to hear."

Earl shrugged. "It happens, right? Multiples are harder."

Cory nodded, making a sympathetic noise in the back of his throat. "How's Wanda?"

"Better. The cast comes off next week."

"This is Eloise. She's a temporary medic."

"Pleasure." Earl shot out a hand and grabbed hers in a firm handshake.

Eloise smiled while the men chatted for a couple of minutes about everything from politics to the running of a ranch. As she listened, she noticed that in the back of the room two tables had been pushed together for a larger party—several members of which were staring directly at her.

Eloise smiled and nodded, looked away. When she glanced back, their attention hadn't moved on. In fact, the last few who hadn't noticed her at first had now joined the rest of the group in eyeing her in undisguised curiosity.

Eloise put a hand on Cory's strong arm, and he paused in his conversation, his gaze following hers.

"Uh-oh."

Eloise looked up at him, her eyebrows rising in surprise. "What do you mean, uh-oh?"

"Come on," he murmured. "Might as well go say hello."

"Can't avoid that one." Earl smirked. "Nice to meet you, Miss."

"Likewise."

Earl ducked behind his coffee cup and made a big show of draining it.

Cory angled a path across the dining room, and Eloise followed his lead. The occupants of the tables in the back turned to their coffee, looking up again only when Cory stopped beside them.

One woman sat in front of a game of solitaire, flipping cards and creating lines with amazing speed, only half her attention on the game. She met Eloise's gaze with a wink.

"Hi, I'm Gloria," she said with a smile.

"Eloise, nice to meet you."

"That you, Cory?" an older woman asked with exaggerated innocence. "Didn't see you come in. How're you?"

She wore her ash-gray hair pulled back in a French braid. Her face had lines from laughter and worry, and her blue eyes sparkled with kindness.

"Hi, Aunt Bea." He bent and kissed her cheek, and she beamed up at him.

"Aren't you going to introduce this young lady?"

"Eloise, this is my family. Everyone, this is Eloise."

Everyone nodded and said their hellos. Eloise looked up at him in surprise, then back at the table of people. He brought her to meet his family?

"Sorry," he murmured. "I didn't think they'd be here. They're supposed to be at a cattle auction."

Two older men scooted down to make room at the table, and a younger man grabbed two chairs from an empty table, depositing them in the newly created gap.

Cory and Eloise sat in the chairs provided and Eloise smiled awkwardly. She was used to diners being filled with disinterested strangers; being surrounded by a table of overly interested strangers was unnerving.

"So." Gloria stopped her flipping and sorting and gave Cory a grin. "How's things?"

The table quieted, and Eloise sensed a whole list of questions lurking beneath the surface of that query.

Cory chuckled. "Not bad. How come you all aren't at the auction?"

She shrugged. "It was rescheduled."

A thin man sitting next to her nodded. "I heard that there are some good stud bulls this time around."

The waitress came by with two fresh coffee cups and handed them over. Her uniform consisted of a yellow pocketed apron on top of jeans and a tee-shirt.

"Coffee?" she asked, a lilt in her voice.

Eloise nodded, and the waitress filled both cups. The coffee smelled good, and she drained two creamer packets into her cup. Everyone at the table seemed to be talking to someone, and she was left mercifully alone for a moment while Cory chatted with Gloria about cattle prices.

"So...Eloise, is it?" an older man said, drawing her attention. He wore a trucker hat with a seed logo emblazoned across the front. "How'd you two meet?"

This question drew the attention of everyone else at the table and their conversations halted midsentence, and Eloise felt heat rise in her cheeks. She glanced at Cory, who shrugged.

"She's standing in as temporary medic," Cory said. "No need to give her the third degree."

"Third degree?" Aunt Bea looked wounded. "Bert was just asking a question."

"How did he find you?" Gloria asked Eloise. "A good medic doesn't come along every day."

Silence fell around the table, and all eyes shifted to Eloise.

"I'm his father's nurse."

"Your father?" Bea said, her voice quiet but carrying.

"What's this, Cory? I didn't think you even knew who your father was."

"I don't want to talk about this." Cory's tone stayed low, but Eloise heard the tension vibrating beneath. She'd said more than she should have, she realized, and she grimaced internally.

"Sorry," she murmured, realizing it was too late now.

"And you're sure he's your father?" Bea shook her head skeptically. "Does this man want something from you?"

"Yes, I'm sure he's my father. And no, he doesn't want anything from me." Cory sighed. "He's dying. I'm taking the opportunity to get to know him."

"So you're taking this man into your home while he dies?" his aunt concluded.

"No. He's only visiting. I wanted to—" Cory cleared his throat. "I only just found out about him. It's complicated."

"So, who is he, exactly?" Bert cut in. "Your mother would never say."

"An accountant in Haggerston. Like I said, I don't want to talk about it."

The silence at the table was almost deafening, and Gloria turned back to her cards, flipping and shuffling, then flipping some more. Her expression was grim.

"I thought your mother warned you away from him," Bea said quietly.

"He doesn't have a lot of time left," Cory replied. "And he's not a danger to anyone right now."

Eloise didn't miss the anger and resentment simmering on the faces of Cory's family. They'd obviously formed their own opinions about Cory's father years ago.

"So, where is he now?" Bert asked, tipping his hat back on his head.

"He's resting at my house, and I'd appreciate a bit of privacy with him. He doesn't need to answer to any of you during his last days."

"He's going to have to answer for a lot more than that when he meets his Maker," Bea muttered.

Cory eyed them, his earlier friendliness hardening. "I figure I need more answers than the rest of you do."

"He's got a point," Bert said, sipping at his coffee. "Don't worry, Cory. We'll give you space. Won't we, Bea?"

"Just don't you trust him." Bea waggled her finger in Cory's direction, tears misting her eyes. "Your mama never did."

"I'm a grown man, Auntie," Cory replied. "I'll be fine. Besides, I've got Eloise here to keep the old guy behaving himself."

"So, what's he like, dear?" Bea asked, turning her attention to Eloise. "You can see how we all feel about him, but you've got professional distance."

"He's my patient, and I can't discuss him," Eloise replied, hoping her words wouldn't offend. No one seemed to take it personally, however, and the conversation reluctantly turned toward other topics.

Eloise glanced up at Cory, and she saw something in his dark gaze that she hadn't expected—a deep sadness. Mr. Bessler's actions had bled far into this family. He was no longer just a neglectful father; he was now an evil legend to the people he'd wounded most personally. She wondered what they saw in their minds when they thought about Cory's father.

"You okay?" Eloise murmured.

Cory's dark eyes met hers, but she saw a distance there. "Sure. I'm fine." He glanced down at his watch and raised his voice to be heard by the rest of the table. "Sorry to dash, everyone."

Cory pushed his chair back and peeled a five off a roll of money from his front pocket, tossing it between their coffee cups. His movement was casual, but Eloise caught the tension in his stance.

"Leaving so soon?" Bea asked, a frown creasing her brow.

"Got to work," he replied with a tight smile. "Still calving over there."

"Well, you take care of him, Eloise."

She nodded and smiled. Cory waved to his family and slid a warm, strong hand behind her back and propelled her through the cafe and toward the door.

"Don't look back," he murmured in her ear. "Or you'll encourage them."

The truck hummed down the highway and Cory draped a hand on top of the steering wheel, the vehicle seeming to know its own way home.

"I'm really sorry I said too much," Eloise said, breaking the silence. "I hadn't realized you were keeping this a secret."

"It's okay." He wasn't angry with her. He was more irritated with himself for not anticipating that whole awkward scene. A fiery curl fell free of her loose ponytail, and it fluttered in the wind of the truck's air-conditioning. Cory had to curb his first instinct to reach out and tuck the curl back, but he pulled his mind away from dangerous territory.

"And you thought I'd been lonely around here." He chuckled. "I'm related to half the county."

"I didn't realize."

He glanced at her again. Eloise was being utterly truthful, he could tell. She was so genuine, so open. The ranching life was probably more culture shock than he'd realized.

"Life out here isn't what you expected, is it?" he asked.

"No." She gave him a sidelong look. "I suppose not. But it's nice."

"Yeah." Cory flicked off the radio, and the music melted away, leaving them in quiet.

"It's different in a city," Eloise said. "You can see hundreds of strangers every day and never recognize a single person." She frowned. "Well, maybe you notice that it's the same guy working at the newspaper stand, but you wouldn't know him."

"Here, you not only know the guy, but you attended his baby's baptism."

"Definitely different. Do you ever wish you had more privacy?"

"What would I do with it?" Cory shrugged, then grinned. "Okay, maybe sometimes. Like today."

"Do you think they'll tell people about your dad?" she asked.

"Only family." When a man was related to as many people as he was in these parts, that didn't mean much.

Fields of green wheat stood on either side of the road. This was Earl's crop. A side road would divide the fields a couple of miles ahead, and that would be the beginning of his own crop. A copse shaded part of the road, and he let his eyes roam down toward Milk River as he passed. Every yard of this land rooted Cory to something bigger—faith, family, community. This land was his livelihood, but it was also part of his soul. His wheat, waving in the summer wind, just looked sweeter, somehow, than his neighbor's.

"So, do you ever get lonely living in the city?" Cory asked.

Eloise laughed bitterly. "I'm a divorced woman whose friends are all married with kids. You better believe I get lonely."

"Did the divorce make a difference?" he asked. "With friendships, I mean."

"Not directly," she admitted. "I'd get invited to a dinner party, but everyone there would come with a spouse. I'd get to know another woman at church, and then she'd find out I'm divorced and that would be the end of that."

Eloise pulled her hair away from her neck. "Well, she'd still be friendly, just more distanced, you know? She'd want to spend the weekend with her husband, and you can't double-date with a single woman. It's that sort of thing."

He nodded. "Your friends must have sided with you over your husband, though."

"Oh, absolutely, and I'm not complaining about my friends. But adjusting to being the divorced one was harder than I thought. It's one of the biggest reasons I took this live-in position with your dad. Haggerston was far enough away from Billings to give me a break."

"Work is always a great excuse, too," he agreed.

Eloise nodded. "You understand."

"Yeah, I do. Being the guy who was left at the altar has a stigma."

"I imagine." She gave him a sympathetic glance. "They haven't forgotten?"

"Have your friends forgotten Philip?" he countered.

"Touché." She stretched out her long legs. "There is a lot to do in a city to take your mind off things, though. The art museum, coffee shops, restaurants, parks, theater…"

"Hmm." Cory attempted to keep his tone neutral. Her list of entertainment possibilities sounded exhausting. He couldn't imagine how fast a person would have to whip through each one to do it all in a month. He'd rather be on his horse or out in a field than trying to fit himself into a suit for museums and galleries. He didn't find healing in crowds; he found it where he could work with his hands and pray. In his experience, God took His time when He answered. God's answers weren't a hundred and forty character tweets—they were breathed on the wind.

"You don't like going to a movie or seeing a play?" Eloise asked.

"We do get movies out here, you know," he teased.

"Do you like opera? Symphonies?" she pressed.

"Do you?"

She was silent for a long moment, her brow furrowed. "It's something to do."

"Really liking something and doing it to fill time are two different things," Cory countered.

"Then I suppose I moderately like those things."

"What do you really like?" he asked.

Eloise didn't answer at first. Emotion flitted across her pale features, and then she shrugged faintly. "I'm still figuring that out after the divorce."

"Fair enough." He glanced over and caught her eye. "At least you know that."

Cory slowed when he saw the Stone Ranch sign approaching, then pulled into the drive. The tires crunched over the gravel, and a twig slapped the windshield as he eased past the lilac bushes.

"You're a wise man," Eloise said quietly.

"Not really," he answered. "I've got time to think is all."

Eloise settled back into the seat as he drove around the familiar turns and headed toward the house. Coming home always felt good, and he remembered the excitement he'd felt as a boy when he and his mother had driven up to the house to visit his grandparents. His grandparents were gone now, of course, but he had his best friend and his wife, and he had his home. But if absolutely pressed, he'd be forced to admit that he was lonely rattling around in that house by himself.

The next day was Sunday, and Cory was a man who prided himself on not missing a service. That was his time away from work, away from the demands of the herds, to connect with God. He glanced over at Eloise.

"I'm going to church tomorrow," Cory said.

"Oh?"

He wondered what she was thinking. Church wasn't exactly a place for privacy, since he was related to half the people who attended. He knew he'd probably regret this tomorrow, but in the moment, all he wanted was a chance to bring her along. He wanted to sit with Eloise in his regular pew and have her next to him instead of sitting there alone thinking about her.

"Do you want to come?" he asked.

A smile sparkled in her eyes. "I could use some church about now."

Cory swung the truck into the parking spot by the house, a smile on his lips, and turned off the engine. "I'm glad you're here, Eloise."

"Me, too." Her gaze moved toward the house. "I should get in and make sure your dad's all right."

"Yeah. Sure. I'll see you later."

Eloise pushed open her door and hopped out of the truck, the scent of her vanilla perfume wafting out after her.

I'd better not be getting used to this, he told himself. When she left and all of this was nothing more than a memory, the last thing he needed was longing for someone already forgetting him.

Chapter Eight

Sunday morning, Eloise sat next to her patient in the back of the little church. Sunlight filtered through stained-glass windows and fell across her lap. The pastor preached from the pulpit, but Eloise's mind was not on the sermon. She was doing some basking—just enjoying the ambience of a quiet Sunday morning in church. The scent of furniture polish and old hymnals mingled with the medicinal smell of her patient sitting next to her.

From his position in his wheelchair in the far aisle next to the towering stained-glass windows, Mr. Bessler stared at the worn carpet, an afghan over his legs. Sitting in church, he seemed tranquil for once, Eloise thought. The stillness seemed to calm him. If the old man needed anything, it was a little bit of serenity.

Eloise glanced back at the thick wooden doors. Still no sign of Cory. He'd driven them there in his truck that morning, then been called away to help an uncle with something. She hadn't caught what was going on. Several people turned to look at Eloise and her patient in open curiosity. One small boy stared over the back of a pew, his round eyes fixed unblinkingly on Mr. Bessler. The old man took no notice.

Father, guide me.

"Thank you." Eloise attempted to face the front once more, but the woman leaned forward again.

"Are you and Cory—" the woman waggled a finger between them, her penciled eyebrows raised questioningly.

"No." Eloise smiled. "Just the medic." She turned around, a laugh rising up inside her. It looked as if the presence of a woman with Cory in a pew also caused a bit of a stir. She wondered what sorts of complications this would cause for Cory later.

Mrs. Burke tapped Eloise's shoulder again.

"He's single," she whispered helpfully.

"Thanks," Eloise replied softly. "But I won't be in town long."

"Oh?"

Mrs. Burke seemed more interested in Eloise than the sermon, and Eloise wondered how she could politely put the woman off.

"Maybe we could talk more after the service," Eloise suggested.

"Oh yes, of course." Mrs. Burke looked mildly offended and leaned back in her seat. Eloise had the vague impression she'd broken a social rule. She glanced at Cory, whose gaze flickered in her direction.

An amused smile flickered at the corners of his lips. "That's Mrs. Burke for you. Local matchmaker extraordinaire."

Eloise idly wondered if Talia Burke's matchmaking was successful or just intrusive, but she didn't ask. Instead she attempted to listen to what the pastor was saying.

A tap on her shoulder drew Eloise's attention once more, and she attempted to veil her annoyance before she turned around.

"Yes?" she whispered.

"I know about your situation," Mrs. Burke whispered. *My situation?* Eloise wondered what the woman meant by that. She could only assume that she was speaking about her position as Mr. Bessler's nurse. *Why can't people just give the man some privacy? Does the entire church have a stake in Cory's paternity?*

"I can't talk about it," Eloise whispered back. "I hope you understand."

"Oh, of course," the older woman crooned. "It would be hard to talk about, but time does heal the wounds, doesn't it?"

"I hope so," Eloise replied. "Thanks for understanding."

Eloise turned around more resolutely this time, but Mrs. Burke hadn't finished. She leaned forward to whisper in Eloise's ear, "Don't think you're the only one, dear. Men can be scoundrels."

Eloise frowned, the sermon forgotten. *What* is *she talking about?*

Eloise turned around. "What do you mean?"

Mrs. Burke scooted to the front of her pew and put a plump hand over Eloise's. "Your husband, of course."

"My..." Eloise's breath caught in her throat.

"I know he ran out on you, but don't let that stop you from living, dear. In fact, I know several single men in this church—"

"No, thank you."

Eloise attempted to smile but wasn't sure if she succeeded or simply bared her teeth at the old woman. She turned back around, heat rising in her cheeks.

How on earth would a random woman in Cory's church know about my divorce? That was the question. She hadn't told anyone except Cory.

Her stomach sank. Had Cory been telling people the things she'd shared with him? It hardly seemed like him, but the fact remained that old Mrs. Burke in the pew behind seemed to be entirely in the know.

So this is what a small community is like, she thought wryly. *Delightful.*

Aunt Bea turned around from her pew near the front of the church, her gaze landing squarely on Mr. Bessler. The old man put out a quivering hand and placed it on Eloise's arm. She leaned toward him.

"Are you okay, Robert?" she whispered.

"Get me out of here." His voice was loud enough to carry, and the pastor stumbled over a few words in his sermon. Eloise inwardly grimaced.

"Okay," Eloise whispered. "But please, Robert, keep your voice down."

Mr. Bessler sank into his chair, averting his gaze.

So he had noticed all the attention. Her heart went out to him. He might not have been a father to speak of, but he was a human being, and when he came to a church to worship, the last thing he needed was judgment.

Attempting to keep her own indignation in check, Eloise released the brake on the old man's chair and wheeled him toward the door.

Cory stepped outside into the warm sunlight, squinting in the brightness. His boots resounded against the wooden steps, and the thick wooden door swung shut behind him, muffling the sound of the preacher's voice.

The Cranton Christian Church was located on a side road across the street from a field of young wheat, rippling in the wind. A barbed-wire fence cradled the bountiful crop that already rose higher than the fence posts. The whitewashed building was topped by a small steeple and a rusted metal cross.

With her back to the church, Eloise stood as if on guard next to his father's wheelchair. Her fiery curls whipped in a rising wind, her black skirt flapping against her legs. She glanced back as Cory walked up.

"I'm sorry about that," Cory said. "They're curious."

"They're judging," his father retorted.

Cory took a deep breath. "All they did was sneak a peek at you. No one said a word."

"No one needed to." The old man looked away. "What did you tell them about me anyway?"

"Me?" Cory bit back a sarcastic retort and attempted to calm the anger sparked inside him. "Do you think no one has thought about you all these years? You're the guy who got my mother pregnant and then dumped her. Don't you think that affected the family?"

"I was married." The old man shrugged his frail shoulders and heaved a wheezing sigh. "What did you want?"

"I know that now, but there were thirty-five years for people to speculate. My extended family helped to raise me when you were out of the picture. You'll have to forgive them for feeling like they have a small stake in this."

"In what?" his father demanded. "A stake in me? I'm no one's business but God's, and I didn't come out here to be a sideshow."

"A stake in you?" Cory shook his head incredulously. "They have a stake in *me*, Robert."

A car cruised past the church, and the three looked toward the vehicle and watched it rumble around a corner. The old man lifted a finger as if about to commence with a lecture, pointing it in Cory's direction.

"I'm not a bad man, Cory." His voice quivered with emotion.

"Maybe not," Cory agreed. "But you've got your faults."

His father nodded slowly. "Fine. But at least I accept my faults. You, on the other hand, think you're a saint. You've never fathered any children. You've never done anything particularly terrible. In fact, I doubt that you've ever done much of anything at all. And you count doing absolutely nothing as a virtue."

"Robert…" Eloise's tone held warning.

"Nothing?" Cory flexed his fists at his sides, indignation fighting to get past his self-control. "What do you call a ranch of my own?"

"An inheritance. You hold on to that land with a death grip, and I think you're afraid to try anything that doesn't involve a field or a herd of cattle."

"And if I went about fathering children and walking away from them, then I'd really have lived?" Cory scoffed. "Is that what you think?"

"I never said I was proud to have fathered you!"

"Robert, that's enough," Eloise snapped. "You know nothing about your son's accomplishments. I've seen how much his employees respect him, and that doesn't come lightly. He's earned my respect, too. He's fair, honest and successful. That's more than most men can boast. So don't say things you don't mean just to be cruel."

Silence swept between them, punctured only by the twitter of birds and the whistle of his father's breathing. Cory looked at Eloise in unveiled surprise. He had no idea she thought so highly of him, and her words buoyed him up in the face of his father's criticism. The old man looked away, his blue eyes snapping in suppressed rage.

"I didn't mean it like that," his father said.

"Then what did you mean?" Cory demanded. "Because I'm perfectly inclined to believe you."

"Your mother was the biggest mistake of my life." Mr. Bessler clenched his teeth. "I never should have started up with her, and not a day has gone by that I haven't regretted that affair."

"My mother?" Cory laughed bitterly. "She's your biggest mistake? A lifetime of lies doesn't factor in there anywhere? You think a short-lived affair was worse?"

"Lies to cover up what I did!" The old man glared at Cory. "I admit I did a terrible thing, but all the lies I told were only to hide the original mistake from my wife. I committed adultery, and it's followed me every day since."

Cory glanced in Eloise's direction and she stood back, that professional reserve on her face again. She was acting the part of the nurse, backing away emotionally, and that distance hurt. But he knew whom he was angry with, and it wasn't Eloise.

"You make my mother sound like some home wrecker, out to destroy your marriage."

"It could have, had my wife found out." His father's lips moved as if he were about to say something more, then he clamped them shut.

"Well, my mother remembered it differently." Cory kicked a pebble, sending it skittering into the grass. "She told me how you charmed her and swept her off her feet. So you're going to tell me that she nearly ruined your life? I think you ruined hers."

"I was weak, and I was stupid." His father's face twisted in distaste. "I was tempted and I will never forgive myself for doing what I did."

"So your answer was to toss her out and walk away from the child you fathered?"

"You were fine."

"How do you even know that?" Cory retorted. "You know nothing about me!"

"She told me...sometimes. She gave me little updates about you."

Cory froze. His mother had been in contact with his father? He'd had no idea. She'd hidden more from him than he'd ever imagined.

"And from that you made the judgment that I was perfectly happy?"

His father remained silent and anger surged up in Cory's chest. This was a conversation to have in private, and for moment, he considered stopping right there. Eloise didn't need to see this. For all he knew, the old man didn't need this conversation, either. Before Cory could decide, he found himself talking again, his tone lower.

"I missed you. I always wondered why you didn't care. Other kids had dads. Other kids had some sort of contact with the man who fathered them, but I never did, and that hurt."

"Well, I'm sorry." The old man shifted in his wheelchair. "I did what was best."

"Well, like my mother I see it differently." Cory turned his back, the fight draining out of him. With the anger seeping away, all that remained was bone-deep exhaustion.

I didn't really want to know this.

It would have been easier never to know his father than to learn the disappointing truth. Somehow his adolescent fantasies about a father with some unknown but excellent excuse to be absent seemed better than this. But there was no going back now. He scrubbed a hand through his hair and turned back. Eloise stood next to the old man, her green eyes locked on Cory as if waiting for a final explosion.

"I'm sorry, Eloise," he said quietly.

She didn't answer, and he wondered what she thought of him in that moment. She'd just seen the worst flying between himself and his father, and while he couldn't think straight about it now, he suspected he'd regret a good deal of it later.

His father stared at a space of grass between Cory and the church; then he slowly raised his gaze to meet his son's. "You were born to the wrong woman, Cory."

"What?" Cory squinted as he regarded the old man hunched before him.

"Ruth wanted a baby more than anything. She prayed every night for a child, and as the years went by, nothing happened. I told her that it was probably my fault. I wanted to believe it as much as she did." He licked his dry lips. "And then—"

"I came along." Cory finished his father's thought.

The old man nodded.

"So if you wanted kids so badly, why not be a father to one you had?"

"I told you. You were born to the wrong woman."

Cory sighed. "I was your Ishmael, and your Isaac never came."

"Something like that."

Cory saw Eloise wrap her arms around her waist and look down at her feet.

"That's fine," he said gruffly. "It is what it is."

"It would have killed her." Tears rose in his father's eyes. "If Ruth had ever known about you, it would have broken her heart beyond repair."

Cory nodded. "So instead you broke my mother's heart and abandoned me."

"The lesser of two evils," the old man murmured.

"You think so?"

From the church, the piano hammered out the opening notes to the closing hymn. Cory glanced at his watch.

"Let's go home," he said and walked purposefully toward his pickup parked across the street. He had no answers. He might very well be out of questions, too, at this point, and all he could think of was getting back home to his ranch where the land was big enough to swallow this ache in his gut.

Eloise pushed Mr. Bessler's wheelchair after Cory. The rancher's shoulders were set. She'd never seen Cory angry before, and she had to admit he was impressive when his ire was up. Mr. Bessler looked down, muttering irritably to himself. Behind them the church door opened, the hymn crescendoed, and then the door banged shut against the music.

"You're Eloise, right?" a girl called from behind them.

A teenage girl hurried across the church lawn, her straight brown hair fluttering out behind her. She waved in Cory's direction.

"Hi, Uncle Cory."

"Hey there, kiddo." Cory's steely gaze softened. "We're just leaving."

"Just wanted to say hi." She grinned. "I'm Kelsie." She offered a hand to Eloise.

"Hi, Kelsie." Eloise smiled and shook the teenager's hand.

"Mom wants me to invite you all for Sunday dinner," Kelsie said.

"Tell your mom thanks for the invite, but we'll be lying low," Cory said.

"Okay." The girl's gaze flickered toward Mr. Bessler, seated in his wheelchair. "Uncle Cory, is this your dad?"

"Yes."

"Can I say hi?"

"No."

Kelsie didn't seem put off by Cory's curt reply. She turned her attention to Eloise. "You know, Uncle Cory hasn't brought a woman around since I was, like, twelve."

Eloise chuckled and shook her head. "I don't count. I'm just his father's nurse."

"Oh yeah?" The girl eyed Eloise speculatively. "Has Uncle Cory told you about Deirdre? She was nice and all, but not right for him."

"Kelsie." Cory's tone held warning. "We're heading home now. You go tell your mom I'll give her a call later, okay?"

Kelsie heaved an exaggerated sigh. "Fine, fine." She

shot Eloise a grin. "You might have noticed that Uncle Cory's hard to nail down, but he's worth it."

"Kelsie!" Cory gave the girl a baleful look, and Kelsie laughed good-naturedly, putting her hands up. She didn't seem the least bit cowed by her uncle's glare.

"I'm leaving, I'm leaving! See you later!"

As Kelsie sauntered back toward the church, her summer dress rippling around her knees in the breeze, Eloise looked askance at Cory. "Your niece?" she asked.

Cory nodded. "Technically my cousin. This is Bea's daughter. And growing up faster than I can keep up with."

"They do that," Eloise agreed with a smile. "She thinks the world of you, though."

Cory grunted and opened the truck door. "Let's just get home."

Chapter Nine

Eloise leaned against the window frame, her gaze trained over the front veranda where Cory stood with his back to the house, his broad, tan hands resting on the wooden rail. Beyond him, bright afternoon sunlight bleached the lawn. Something in the set of his wide shoulders spoke of heaviness. Down the hallway, Mr. Bessler snored softly.

Eloise considered slipping away to leave Cory to his thoughts, but she paused, her eyes lingering on the tall cowboy. They'd gotten closer over the past few days, and whether he'd wanted her to or not, she'd witnessed some of his toughest moments with his father. It wasn't his relationship with his dad that was nagging her, though—it was the old woman who knew a bit too much about her personal life. Eloise had a sense that perhaps she'd misplaced her trust, and while she once would have done anything to avoid confrontation, she was older and wiser now. Besides, she couldn't be certain of Cory's betrayal until she heard his side of it. She stood undecided for several moments; then before she could regret her decision, she opened the door and stepped outside.

Cory turned.

"Hi," she said quietly.

"That was an interesting Sunday, huh?" He gave her a wry smile.

"You could say that." She tucked a stray curl back into the loose bun at the back of her head.

"I'm really sorry," he said again, turning back to face the sunny lawn. "I probably should have left well enough alone with my dad."

"You had a conversation with your father—one that was long overdue, I think. You have nothing to apologize for. I wanted to ask you about something else."

"Oh?" Cory turned to face her again.

"That woman who was talking to me in the service— she said she'd heard about my situation."

"What situation?" He frowned.

"My divorce. She'd heard that my husband left me."

Color drained from Cory's face. "How?"

"She didn't say, but—" Eloise sighed. "You're the only one I told, Cory, and I told you as a friend. I didn't think you'd gossip about it."

"I didn't!" He sighed. "Wait—"

The hesitance in his tone gave her pause, and her stomach sank. She didn't know what explanation she was hoping for, but she wanted it to prove him innocent of talking to someone about her most personal failure. Eloise attempted to hide her misgiving and raised an eyebrow.

"Look, I was talking to Zack, and it came up."

Came up? All the hope she had for a marvelous explanation seeped out of her, leaving behind a bedrock of disappointment. A curl tickled her forehead and she batted it back.

"How?" she asked after a moment. "I don't get how my personal life became a topic of discussion with your partner."

Color rose in Cory's face and he rubbed a hand over his eyes. "Zack was suggesting that you and I could—"

he shrugged faintly "——be something more. You know him and Nora, always trying to set me up. I told him that I didn't think it would work."

"Because my husband left me," she concluded. He nodded, and she sighed. He was right that it wouldn't work. She was nowhere near being able to trust a man again. If Philip could dupe her so completely, she'd have to be stupid to hand her heart over to someone else.

Cory nodded. "I'm sorry. I should have kept my mouth shut. It was wrong of me."

"So that's how places this size work, huh?" Eloise attempted a tight smile. "Say one thing and it spreads like wildfire?"

Cory shook his head. "Pretty much. You breathe a word and someone else breathes a word and before you know it——"

"Strange women are accosting me in church?"

He shrugged apologetically. "It won't happen again. I feel terrible. Can you forgive me?"

"I suppose so," she said with a faint smile. "You're turning out to be a pretty decent friend."

Cory reached across the railing to put his warm hand over hers. "Thanks."

Eloise turned her hand over in his gentle grip and squeezed his in return. She might not be ready for romance yet—she might not ever—but she could certainly appreciate a solid friend in her life right now. All she wanted was to lie low and lick her wounds for a while longer.

"It's this place." Eloise looked over the lawn, and the grazing horses beyond. "There is no way to just blend into a wall, is there?"

"Not really. There are good things about a small, tight-knit community, though." He released her hand, and she reluctantly pulled it back. "But privacy isn't one of them." Cory gave her a wry smile. "And if it makes you feel any better, that whole conversation I had with my father in front of the church will probably be repeated verbatim to everyone I know within hours."

Eloise smiled. Deep down, in a small petty part of her, it did make her feel a little better, but she wouldn't admit to that.

"Are you sure you don't want that privacy?" she asked instead.

"I have people who care. That counts for more. Besides, if I want privacy, I can get on a horse and ride."

"It makes a cold, faceless city a whole lot more appealing right now," she said.

"Is my dad okay?" he asked, changing the subject.

"He's asleep."

Cory sighed and leaned back against the rail, crossing his arms over his broad chest. "I hadn't realized how much he resented me."

A soft breeze lifted Eloise's curls away from her face, bringing with it the scent of lilacs. "That wasn't the truth. Not all of it." She shook her head. "Your father threw around a few facts and some opinions. The truth is always broader and deeper than that."

"What makes you so sure?"

Eloise shrugged. "Call it a gut instinct. He came out here because he wanted to know you, too."

"It's okay, Eloise. I don't need to have a warm and fuzzy moment with my dad."

"And you might not get one," she replied frankly. "But you also don't have to accept a five-minute argument as the whole truth about a very complicated situation."

She met his gaze and he squinted back at her. His dark hair shifted in the breeze, and for a moment, she thought he wouldn't answer. Then a smile toyed at one side of his mouth.

"You are strangely wise, Eloise."

She chuckled. "I have time to think, too."

Cory turned back toward the yard. Mr. Bessler had hurt him more than the old man would ever know. Her patient irritated her sometimes with his crustiness, too, but her expectations were much lower. Eloise sighed.

"He's not a great father, I'll give you that. And only Ruth knows what kind of husband he made. He's cantankerous, opinionated and stubborn. But he's also an excellent friend."

"I guess that's good for his friends," Cory replied. "You weren't related to him."

"Maybe you could try to get to know him on a different level. He's not going to meet expectations as a father, but there is good in him."

"Why do you defend him?" Cory asked.

"Because somebody has to," she replied. "He's not all bad, and I've learned to really like him. He's facing his own mortality, and that's not easy for anyone. I think he could use a little grace."

"Fair enough." Cory nodded.

A gray cat sauntered across the lawn, tail in the air, drawing Eloise's gaze along with it. The feline slipped off into a ditch.

"So, what about you, then?" Cory asked.

"What about me?"

"What about your parents?"

"My dad and I are pretty close. My mom died when I was fourteen in a car accident, so after that it was just the two of us."

"Is he still alive?"

"He's in Billings," she said. "He runs a small used bookstore. It's his retirement project."

Cory smiled wistfully. "It sounds nice. Do you talk to him often?"

Eloise nodded. "I give him a call every couple of days.

Normally he's sorting books, and he stops to chat. When I lived in Billings, I used to drop by the store and take him out for a coffee. He'd close up shop and we'd go to the corner coffee joint and just talk for a while. I miss him."

"Now, that's a good father," Cory said soberly.

"We never get the perfect lot in life," Eloise replied. "I had a great father who adored me, but I lost my mom when I needed her most. We all just do our best with what we've got."

"I suppose so."

Eloise's gaze swung from the horse barn and up the dusty road until the copse hid the rest from sight.

"Look, I know I didn't have it as badly as you did—" she began.

"Don't worry about it. I survived." His warm eyes moved slowly over her face. He stepped closer, his dark eyes pulling her in. A stray curl fluttered in her vision. Cory caught it and wrapped the tendril slowly around his finger. A smile tugged at his lips as he tucked the curl gently behind her ear. She tipped her head back to meet his gaze, and as he looked down into her face, his eyes filled with tenderness.

Is he about to—

She dared not finish the thought, but he leaned closer, and the intensity of the moment tugged her in.

From inside the house, Robert's thin voice called out, "Red?" Cory paused, pressed his lips together. He pulled back.

"Well." He pushed himself away and cleared his throat. "I've got to go check on the horses."

"Okay." Her voice sounded breathless, even in her own ears.

Cory grabbed his hat from the railing and dropped it on his head with the resoluteness of a man leaving for a month. Then he glanced back at her. "I'll be in the horse barn. Why don't you bring my dad over?"

Eloise nodded, trying to calm the patter of her heart. "Sure."

"And wear some boots. Nora left some for you in the mudroom. I want to show you the alternative to that cold, private city. I think you'll like it."

Without a backward glance, Cory trotted down the stairs and strode across the lawn. Eloise leaned against a post and rubbed a hand over her eyes.

"You're here for Robert," she reminded herself. "Don't forget that."

The horse barn was a long building, lined with horse stalls, now mostly empty. Dust motes danced through a ray of sunlight slanting through a window by the saddles and tack. Burnished leather shone in warm tones, and rows of bridles hung limply along another wall. The scent of horses and fresh hay wafted through the length of the building, following a cross breeze. A couple of ranch hands had already finished mucking out the place, and Cory stood next to his horse. She was a strawberry roan Arabian with a small head and delicate feet. At fifteen, she was middle-aged and calm. The silence was broken only by the swishing of Lexie's tail and the drone of a fly bouncing off a windowpane.

"Lord, I'm such an idiot," Cory muttered, sliding the currycomb over Lexie's flank. She stamped her hoof in pleasure. "Give me some self-control here, Father. I'm running low."

Or maybe his father's call for his nurse had been providential. He'd almost kissed Eloise on the porch, and he could only hope she hadn't noticed. Kissing her wasn't part of the plan, but if it hadn't been for the old man's interruption, he wouldn't have stopped himself. He saw something in her—something more than the city girl—and he wanted to show her what a ranch could offer.

"She's no cowgirl, Lexie," he said quietly. The horse swung her head back, nuzzled his arm, then went back to her oats. Lexie probably understood him better than any woman ever had.

"You get that, don't you?" he asked. ·

The horse's muscles shivered as the coarse bristles moved over her coat. Lexie turned her head to look at him again, her big eyes regarding him with the soulful compassion only a horse can manage.

"Yeah, you get it." He chuckled, and moved around to her other side to continue grooming. "You're a good listener, old girl."

She nickered in response.

"Now, I want you to be polite, Lexie. She's a new rider, and she doesn't know her boot from her backside. So you be nice, okay?"

Lexie put her nose into her oats again and Cory shrugged. Lexie was his first choice when letting kids ride. She was intuitive and gentle, and he had no doubt she'd ease Eloise into the riding experience admirably, but he tried to dampen his hopes with a cold dose of reality. A canter through a field didn't make a cowgirl.

After saddling Lexie, Cory led her out into the yard next to Winner, the black stallion he planned to ride, who stood sedately, saddled and ready to go. Winner was less accommodating and more willful, but he needed the riding time to curb some of his bad habits, and there was no time like the present to give him some much-needed practice.

"Heading out for a ride?" Zack called, ambling up to the fence.

"I thought I'd take Eloise around the paddock on Lexie."

Zack grinned. "Winner's been testy today. He tried to bite Nora when she brought him hay this morning."

Cory chuckled. "Thanks for the heads-up."

"So, where's Eloise?" Zack asked.

Cory jutted his chin in the direction of the house. Eloise was already on her way down the drive, pushing his father's chair. Her cheerful voice filtered toward them as she chatted with the old man, her words blending in with the wind.

"Did you mention Eloise's situation to anyone, Zack?" Cory asked.

"I told Nora about it."

Cory nodded.

"Why?" Zack inquired.

"Never mind." The damage was already done. Cory couldn't blame his friends for his own lack of discretion. "I was just going to take Eloise around the paddock where Robert could watch us, but if you'll be around for a bit, maybe you could hang out with my father while I take her out for a decent ride. What do you say?"

Zack shrugged and grinned. "Sure."

"Thanks." Cory pointedly ignored his friend's mirth and waved to Eloise as she approached. "Go through the barn!" he called to her. She waved back and adjusted her course.

"You know, I thought Nora was all wrong for me, too," Zack commented.

"Yeah, and you were dead wrong." Cory chuckled.

"You could be, too, you know."

"Dead or wrong?" Cory joked.

Zack shot him a mildly amused look. "Laugh it up, man, but when you've tasted married life, there's no going back."

"I'm blissfully ignorant of everything I'm missing," Cory retorted.

Zack laughed and patted Lexie's rump on his way by. "Have it your way, but a girl like her doesn't come along every day."

Don't I know it! Cory thought. He took the horses by

their reins and led them toward the barn door, arriving just as Eloise and his father did. Eloise took a step back in alarm.

"Don't worry," Cory said. "They're gentle."

"Scared of a horse?" his father teased.

Color rose in Eloise's cheeks. "Can I pet them?" she asked.

"This is Lexie." Cory led the smaller horse forward. "You can pet her nose and get to know her a little bit."

Eloise reached forward tentatively, and Lexie met her halfway, accepting a stroke along her muzzle. A smile sparkled in Eloise's eyes.

"Well, aren't you pretty?" she murmured.

"That's a nice stallion you've got there," his father said, nodding at Winner.

"Yeah, he's a good horse, but he needs more time."

"He's a biter, isn't he?" the old man asked.

"How'd you know?"

"Just a suspicion. He's got that look in his eye." He eyed the horse warily. "Soldier was just like him. Stubborn and angry, that beast."

"A complicated relationship," Cory said, and the old man laughed, meeting Cory's gaze with a humored look.

"We were both old cranks. We got along fine."

"I don't imagine you'd be able to ride?" Cory asked.

His father shook his head. "I'll watch. It'll do. You'll have your hands full with that one."

Cory wasn't sure if the old man was referring to Winner or Eloise, and he chose not to clarify.

"We won't be too long," Cory said, and when his father gave him a silent nod, he caught Eloise's eye. "You ready?"

"For what, exactly?"

"Back in Haggerston, you said all you needed was a good teacher." He shot her a grin. "Well, you've got one."

"You want to teach me to ride?"

"You want to learn?"

"Oh, go on," his father said. "You'll like it."

Eloise glanced up at Cory, her eyes sparkling in excitement. "All right. How do I do this?"

Cory handed Winner's reins to Zack and led Lexie to a mounting box beside the fence. Eloise walked beside him, hot summer wind blowing through her thick curls.

Cory caught her hand in his and smirked at the surprise in her widened eyes. "Okay, so you're going to put your foot in this stirrup here and get a hold of the saddle horn."

Eloise stepped onto the mounting block and lifted her leg up, but the reach wasn't an easy one, even for an experienced rider.

"You're pretty small," Cory noted, catching her around the waist as she got her boot into position. "Ready?"

She reached toward the back of the saddle—a common first instinct.

"It might look harder, but grab the horn—the front—of the saddle." Eloise reached for the horn and Cory lifted her slight weight upward as she stretched.

"Swing that leg over," he commanded, and Eloise landed on Lexie's back with a gasp of surprise. "See?" Cory swung the reins over Lexie's ears and placed them in her hands. "Easy as pie."

"What do I do?" she asked breathlessly.

"Sit there." He chuckled and went to get Winner from where he stood with Zack and the old man.

"Don't mind saying," the old man muttered, "that woman looks good on a horse."

Cory glanced back. Eloise sat atop Lexie's golden back, her fiery curls already working loose from her ponytail. With her sparkling eyes and skin as pale as new milk, he couldn't help the smile that came to his lips. She reached forward and stroked Lexie's neck cautiously.

"Yeah, she sure does." Cory took the reins from his

friend, tipped his hat to the men, then swung up onto Winner's back. Winner took several steps as he mounted—another bad habit to curb, Cory thought. He tugged the reins and guided the stallion back toward Eloise and Lexie.

"I'll lead the way," Cory said. "Just follow me."

He squeezed Winner's sides and angled toward the gate. Zack trotted across the yard to open it.

"How?" Eloise called.

"Squeeze with your knees," he said. "You've probably seen this on TV."

Eloise complied, but Lexie was less than cooperative.

"Lexie!" Cory called, command in his tone. "Get a move on!" He made a clicking sound with his mouth and the mare obediently walked after Cory. When she caught up, Cory shot Eloise a grin. "She knows you're a newbie. You've got to show her who's boss."

"I think she knows exactly who's boss," Eloise answered.

Cory and Winner led the way to the gate, where Zack stood back, holding it open for them. He met Cory's gaze with a mischievous grin and flicked the brim of his hat in a salute. The horses sauntered through.

"See you in a while," Zack called, and the gate clicked shut behind them.

Green field spilled open before them, rolls and dips of endless ripples as the wind strummed the grass with invisible fingers. Sunlight shone brightly, and the shadow of clouds slipped over the fields in the distance. The stress and pressures of life melted off Cory's shoulders. He reined Winner back as he pawed at the ground in anticipation and Cory turned to catch Eloise's eye. She stared out at the scene before them, her lips parted, and eyes bright. He knew that feeling all too well.

"You ready?" he asked.

Chapter Ten

Cory was a patient teacher, showing her how to guide the horse, lean back into the saddle, and let her hips move with the rolling gate of Lexie's body. It felt counterintuitive to sit and let the horse simply go, but when Eloise complied, her balance returned. The sensation of trusting an animal's step was reminiscent of a ride on her father's shoulders when she was young. She remembered how her father would tease her, pretending to trip, and the way her heart would leap.

"Daddy, be careful!"

"Not so hard, right?" Cory asked.

Eloise grinned. "I think I'm getting the hang of it."

"Come on, this way."

Cory reined his horse left and they moved over the rolling land in a slow canter. Green grass stretched before them, sliced in two by a dusty dirt road in the distance. Golden afternoon sunlight warmed her shoulders. The scent of grass swam along the breeze and Eloise shook her head, letting the wind work through her curls.

"So this is what you do when you need space?" Eloise called ahead.

Cory slowed his horse until he was beside hers. The

soft plod of hooves made a soothing rhythm, and Eloise caught his dark gaze on her.

"I normally take this ride alone," he said.

A smile touched her lips. "I can see why."

The golden sunlight caressed the lush fields, and from the crest of a gentle swell, Eloise spotted cattle far in the distance. She felt tiny on this vast landscape, the sky almost swallowing them.

"There's something about big, open spaces that lets me feel more," Cory said. "I don't have to be so careful out here."

"Careful about what?" she asked, shading her eyes with one hand to better see his face.

"I'm a big guy." He shrugged. "If I get upset—" He looked away. "Well, you know what I mean. You've seen me angry. I learned pretty early that when you're bigger than everyone else, you've got to be gentler than they are, too."

"So you're always reining it in?" she asked.

"Not always. But when I am upset, I come out here. There's no one to offend, or scare."

"You didn't scare me when you and your father hashed things out this morning, and you didn't offend me, either."

"No?" He laughed, the sound low and warm. "I'm glad of that."

She couldn't imagine being afraid of Cory. He was big, and he was most certainly strong, able to toss her up on a horse without much effort at all, but with his strength came tenderness, too.

They rode in silence for a few minutes, and Eloise's thoughts settled on this muscular cowboy, quietly attempting to make sense of him. His dark eyes moved over the landscape with easy familiarity. The reins hung loosely in his broad hands, and she couldn't help wondering what made him worry about scaring people. Something must have happened, she imagined, something that made him wary of expressing his emotions without restraint.

"Whom did you scare?" she asked quietly.

"Hmm?" He glanced over.

"You must have scared someone at some point. Who was it?"

Cory didn't seem inclined to answer at first; then after a moment, he said, "My cousin."

Winner shook his head restlessly, then eyed Lexie. Cory tugged the reins, easing the stallion away. They fell into silence again, and Winner shook his head a few more times, trying to launch into a gallop, but Cory held him back. When the horse finally gave up, Cory moved closer to Eloise once more.

"Behave yourself, Winner." Cory sighed. "You're not looking very nice in front of the lady, you know."

"What happened with your cousin?" Eloise asked as Lexie danced a few steps away from the other horse.

"We were both about sixteen. I had a crush on a girl at school and I'd almost worked up my courage to ask her out. Then my cousin swept in and asked her first." He shrugged. "It sounds silly now, but it mattered a lot then. I was furious. It wasn't like I hit him, even though I probably did consider it, but when I was angry—I saw the look of terror on his face."

"Well, he had it coming," she said.

"Deserved or not, I didn't want to see that look in anyone's face again. So then and there, I asked God to help me control my temper. I took my feelings out here to deal with them."

"I can't imagine you that mad," she said.

"I'd like to keep it that way." Humor sparkled in his eyes.

Eloise looked away. This conversation was getting personal—all her own fault, of course. She'd been the one to go down this avenue with him. She sucked in a deep breath. Cory was a friend, she reminded herself, and his deepest emotions weren't really her business, no matter how much she might want to know. She had to bring things back to a more casual level, and quickly.

"In my line of work, I have to be calm, collected and professional constantly. My patients and their families are dealing with grief. They don't need my feelings to complicate things. So I think I get it. Sometimes we have to protect others."

There, that should do it, she thought in satisfaction.

"I hope you don't lump me in with that group of people."

Eloise glanced toward him. "Of course I do. You're my patient's son."

"I'm different. I barely know my father."

"That doesn't change the fact that you'll have an emotional response to his passing," she replied quietly.

"Sure I will." Cory nodded slowly, his gaze fixed on the countryside. "But that doesn't mean I'm not strong enough to handle the real you, either."

Eloise felt a jerk and she heaved forward. She clutched at a handful to mane to keep from catapulting into the grass and she sucked in a breath, her heart hammering as she regained her balance.

"Careful, Lexie," Cory said. He looked at the ground behind them. "She stepped into a hole."

Eloise nodded, then laughed breathily. "I'm not used to this."

She released her grip on the horse's tough mane. "Sorry, Lexie. I hope that didn't hurt."

"Oh, a tug on her mane won't hurt her," he said. "You're doing well. You've got a good instinct."

A rush of warmth passed over her at his compliment. The group of trees drew closer, and Eloise wiped moisture from her forehead. A bee buzzed up from the grass, circled her head and then droned off again. Cory's horse stamped impatiently.

"Easy, Winner." Cory's tone stayed low but commanding. "We're taking it easy today."

"He wants to run?"

Cory nodded. "He's still learning to listen to me. This is good practice for him. He's getting better, but training a horse takes time and patience. It's a relationship as much as a job."

The trees were coming up quickly, and Eloise wiped the back of her hand over her moist forehead.

"Too hot?" Cory asked.

She nodded. "I could use some shade."

Cory made a click with his mouth and eased Winner toward the trees. Lexie fell into line behind, the two horses finally seeming to cooperate with each other.

"After we cool off, we should head back," Cory called over his shoulder.

Time to go back. The words brought a wave of responsibility. Eloise couldn't stay out here in the fields all day. She had a patient waiting for her. Eloise straightened her spine, enjoying the cool touch of the breeze through her shirt, and the shade of the overhanging branches was a relief. She wiped her forehead and looked around.

Before she had a chance to enjoy the view, a *crack* tore through the quiet, and Winner reared up, the massive horse pawing the air. Winner's hooves, his tossing mane and Cory on his back, reins clutched in his fists, were the last thing Eloise saw before she felt herself whirled around. She lurched backward as Lexie broke into a gallop. The movement nearly tore Eloise right off Lexie's back, but somehow her feet stayed in the stirrups. Her hair whipped around her face, blinding her as she bent forward, clutching at anything she could hold on to.

Lexie bolted across the field, her feet thundering beneath her, and for a split second Eloise felt herself falling—or perhaps flying. Then Lexie's feet hit the ground once more, speeding her across the verdant fields toward the distant barn.

Oh, God, she prayed desperately, *don't let me fall!*

Cory grabbed the reins and pushed up in the stirrups as Winner reared. A falling branch and a leaping hare had been the culprits for this spook, and it took all of his strength to stay on the stallion's back. Winner shook his mane and whinnied, and by the time he hit the ground, Cory took control of the reins once more. Horses were like anyone else—you couldn't reason with them when they were upset.

Winner took a full circle, and as he came around, Cory saw the empty space of grass where Eloise had been. He whipped his head around and spotted her—the back of her, at least—disappearing across the field, Lexie in full gallop.

"Oh no…" Cory heeled Winner into motion and they catapulted across the field in pursuit.

"You wanted to gallop," Cory muttered through gritted teeth.

Winner stretched out to his full length as he thundered across the field. Cory crouched low over the stallion's back, balanced on the stirrups, as those hooves drummed so loudly that he could feel it in his chest. Winner might not listen well, but that horse could run!

The gap between Eloise and Cory slowly closed. Lexie was tiring, her pace slowing, but Winner still ran strong. The barn loomed closer than ever, and Cory steered Winner closer to Lexie. The smaller horse darted away as he made a reach for the reins, and Cory breathed a prayer.

Eloise clung to the horse's mane with a white-knuckled grip.

"Eloise!" Cory shouted, and she turned wide, panicked eyes toward him.

Lexie swerved again, and Cory eased Winner back toward them. Lexie was headed home—that much was certain. The barn loomed, and he knew that if he didn't stop her soon, she'd either break a leg in a gopher hole or hurl Eloise from her back when she tried to stop. With one more swipe, he grabbed Lexie's reins and tugged her closer to Winner's side.

He guided both horses into a large circle, slowing them to a trot, their sides heaving.

Eloise was trembling from head to toe.

"You okay?" he asked.

She didn't reply. *Not a good sign.*

Cory swung off Winner's back and let the horse wander off a few paces. He stroked Lexie's neck and gave her some reassuring pats.

"Come here." Cory held up his arms to Eloise, and she accepted his help in getting off Lexie's back. Her hands shook as she placed them on his shoulders. When Eloise's feet hit the ground, her knees buckled.

"Hey, keep breathing," he said, holding her close against his side as she regained her footing. He put a finger under her chin to get a better look at her blanched face. "You look pretty scared."

She nodded, sucking in a deep breath. "I'm okay."

"That's called a spooked horse, by the way."

"Good to know." She pushed her wild curls away from her face. "I thought I'd fall off and get trampled."

"Feel better now?" Cory glanced at the barn. It was still a fair distance from where they stood. "Do you think you could ride the rest of the way home?"

Eloise shot him an incredulous look. "Not a chance. I'm walking."

Cory shrugged and collected the reins of both horses to walk them. Eloise set off ahead of him, tramping through the deep grass. Her tangled curls fluttered out behind her.

"Wait for us," Cory called.

She slowed her pace and looked back at him. "What on earth happened out there?"

"A dead branch broke from a tree, and a hare jumped in front of Winner at the same time. It startled him. I guess Winner's spook set off Lexie. When they're scared, they run for home."

Eloise rubbed her face. "I'm going to leave the leisurely Sunday afternoon rides to you from now on."

"Oh, come on," he cajoled. "It was scary, but you did great. You're a natural when it comes to riding."

"I don't care," she retorted. "Nothing felt natural about that."

She plowed on ahead, stepping high to make her way through the grass.

"Are you mad at me?" he asked.

Eloise turned, her snapping green eyes meeting his. "I'm furious."

"It wasn't my fault. You have to know that."

"I didn't say I was mad at you. I said I was mad." She arched an eyebrow as if that proved something, but she waited as he caught up.

"Fair enough," he said, scooping up her hand in his.

"I'm fine." She tugged her hand free, but as she did so, her foot dropped into a gopher hole. She went down with a squeak. Cory caught her under one arm and helped her back up.

"Come on," he said, taking her hand once more. "Let's get you home."

Eloise consented to hold his hand, leaning on him when the ground dipped unexpectedly, and Cory tightened his arm, gently lifting her back up. She didn't weigh much, and he glanced down more than once, trying to decipher what lay under that brittle anger. The horses plodded co-operatively after them, no sign that they'd just bolted for the barn minutes before, except for the gloss of sweat on their sides.

"So probably not the best introduction to horseback riding," Cory commented.

"Don't worry about it," she replied. "I should be working anyway."

"It's Sunday. Don't you ever rest?"

Eloise didn't seem in the mood for banter. She marched on, and when they reached the gate, she tugged her hand free.

"Do you think you'll give it another try one of these days?" he asked.

Why did he find himself filled with fragile hope when he asked that?

"No."

"Hey." He touched her arm. "Why are you so upset?"

Tears misted Eloise's eyes and she blinked them back. "It's better than crying." Her chin trembled, and Cory pulled her against his chest. She crumpled handfuls of his shirt into her fists as she sniffled into his chest. Then she pulled back and wiped her eyes.

"Sorry about that," she said. "I'm done now."

"That scared you pretty bad, huh?" he asked.

She wiped the last of the tears from her cheeks with the flat of her palms. "That's the last time I ride a horse."

Cory led the horses toward the barn door and Eloise beelined toward the fence where Robert and Zack waited.

A spooked horse made her cry.

He could hear the guffaws of the ranch hands already—if he chose to tell the story. They loved a good city slicker yarn, and Eloise seemed like the perfect heroine for countless tales of inept city people trying to do the basics on a ranch.

He couldn't tell it, though. He knew that already. She

might not be much of a cowgirl, but she didn't deserve to be mocked.

Don't fall for her, you idiot, Cory chided himself, and he turned away from her receding form, those fiery curls whipping in the wind, and led the horses into the dim, dusty barn.

"Lexie," he murmured. "You should have known better than that."

Yet somehow blaming the horse seemed too easy.

It wasn't Lexie's fault, and it wasn't Eloise's, either. It was his, for having expected something that he never should have hoped for.

He could hear his mother's voice echoing in his head: *"Let people be who they are, son. You can't change them, so it hurts less if you don't expect it to happen."*

She'd been referring to his father at the time, but it seemed to apply to his father's intriguing nurse, too.

Tossing his hat onto a nail on the wall, Cory stroked Lexie's neck. As he unbuckled the saddle, a prayer rose in his heart. *Why am I doing this to myself, Father? Guide me, and take away this—whatever this is I'm feeling for her.*

Because right now, it would take some divine intervention to make him stop falling for her.

Chapter Eleven

Eloise shut her bedroom door and locked it. Mr. Bessler and Cory had had her in the middle of too many of their conversations, and Eloise thought it was time they were alone, so she made an excuse that she needed a little rest and escaped to the bedroom. From the kitchen, Cory's voice rumbled, low and kind. She couldn't make out words, but his presence was comforting somehow.

Outside the window, dark clouds slid in slowly, thunder rumbling far in the distance, and the scent of rain slipped in through the cracked window. She paused, watching the daylight dim as the storm threatened. It always amazed her how quickly a storm could sweep across Montana, but when she was in the city, she didn't get the same view because of the buildings. Out here there was nothing between them and the ferocity of nature. Eloise sank onto the side of her bed, embracing the luxury of solitude with her aching muscles that were already protesting the horseback ride.

The round mirror atop the mahogany dresser reflected her face. The soft angle of her collarbone was the only part visible. Eloise pulled her hair back and looked at the makeup-free face. Life was not easy. It had proven harder for her than for many of her friends, she knew. But even with the bumps and bruises of the past few years, Eloise liked herself better now.

She ran her fingers over her pale cheekbones, noting the slight discoloration under her eyes.

I need more rest.

Eloise turned away from the mirror and leaned back against the bed, heaving a sigh. Horseback riding looked so peaceful and serene on TV. In books, it sounded exhilarating. In real life, just like the rest of her life, the experience left much to be desired.

Marriage was supposed to be happy. Hers ended miserably.

Friends were supposed to embrace her no matter what happened in her life, but her divorce made a lot of those relationships awkward.

Love was supposed to come along and make everything easier, but when she met a man who intrigued her for the first time since Philip left, there was nothing simple about it.

If she had to be honest with herself, Cory did fascinate her. He was strong, confident... Dare she admit how handsome he was?

Eloise eased herself around so that she could lay her head on the pillow, her thigh muscles on fire.

"It doesn't matter if he's handsome," she reminded herself softly.

This was a man who lived his life with land and cattle. She was a woman who painted pictures and shopped at farmers' markets in the city. She couldn't help who she was. She couldn't help who he was, and she definitely couldn't help that they weren't right for each other.

Ironically, that seemed to be the one thing that hadn't changed in her life—not being the right woman.

Lord, why can't I just get over this pain and move on with my life?

From the kitchen, she heard the hum of her patient's voice interspersed with Cory's bass tones.

"Be realistic, Eloise," she murmured. "This isn't your life."

This wasn't her bedroom, and it wasn't her land. And in a matter of days, she'd never be introduced to these particular muscles again.

Cory glanced out the window at the gathering storm. Wind whipped by the buildings, moaning eerily, and he flicked on the radio, waiting for a weather report. So far, it was just talk radio. He turned down the volume.

"Do you want some tea, sir?" he asked.

The old man shrugged. "Sure."

Cory looked in the direction Eloise had gone.

"You've got a thing for my nurse," his father said, chortling.

Cory ignored the comment, grabbing a couple of tea bags instead.

"I know her better than you do," the old man went on.

"I don't want to talk about her," Cory replied.

"Sure you do. You just don't want to talk about her *with me*." His father raised an eyebrow. "Am I right?"

Cory crossed his arms over his chest and regarded the old man. Robert was trying to get a rise out of him. What he hoped to gain, he had no idea. Earlier today, Cory thought he'd almost had a bonding moment with his father over the horses. Now the old man seemed more interested in baiting him.

"She's a good nurse and you're fortunate she's stuck around," Cory said instead. "Frankly, I'm surprised you haven't run her off yet." He gave his father a teasing grin. If his father wanted to bait someone, he'd just met his match.

"I'm cuter than you think," he retorted. "So, what's holding you back from asking her out?"

"None of your business."

"Fine." The old man shrugged.

Cory filled two mugs with steaming water from the kettle and dropped the teabags on top. He slid one across the table to his father, sending a sugar bowl after it.

"My mother never told me much about you," Cory said.

"What is there to tell?" He spread his hands. "I was an accountant. I was married. I never was much to look at."

"What about horses?" Cory asked. "I've got a soft spot for Winner. He sounds a lot like Soldier."

"I would have trusted that horse with my life," his father said softly. "Mind you, I wouldn't have trusted him not to bite me. Just not to kill me."

Cory grinned. "I know that feeling."

"Eloise doesn't seem to be a fan of horses, though."

"That was her first ride."

"And probably her last."

The old man was likely right, and Cory resented his accuracy. It shouldn't matter at this point, but the fact stung, like a personal failure. Cory shrugged. "I don't want to talk about Eloise. It's not right to discuss her behind her back."

"Why? You want me to talk about my life and my personal things, but you don't want to talk about the woman you've been making cow eyes at for the last week. It's hardly fair."

"I'm not making cow eyes at her."

"But you're attracted to her."

"Robert, seriously, leave her out of this."

The old man shot him an irritated look. "What are we supposed to talk about, then? Our warm family memories?"

"Look, you weren't much of a father. I've accepted that. Let's just move on. Maybe get to know each other."

"Like friends?" his father demanded. "Am I really the

kind of man you'd spend time with if you weren't related to me?"

Cory rubbed a hand over his eyes. "Okay, fine. We'd never spontaneously become friends otherwise, but here we are. Let's just make the best of this. We've had some time together, and it hasn't killed us yet."

"Tell me about your mother," the old man said. "I'm curious about her life, what became of her."

"What do you want to know?" Cory asked.

"Was she happy?"

"No," he replied honestly. Images of his mother swam through his mind, and most of them were of a woman with brooding eyes and a sad smile. His most vivid memory of her was her looking out the kitchen window, her expression somber and her arms crossed over her chest protectively. She tried to be cheerful for Cory, but he hadn't been fooled.

The old man frowned. "I thought she would have had a good life. She was the positive sort."

"She was melancholy, thoughtful." Cory sifted through his memories for an efficient description of his mother. "She was sad a lot."

"She wasn't like that when I knew her. She was bubbly. Fun."

"If she was, it was before my time," Cory replied. "I don't remember her any other way."

"Oh, pshaw!" He shook his head. "I don't believe that."

"I don't care if you do. You asked, and I answered." The old man's flippancy bugged him. Who did he think he was to brush off a woman's misery?

"And you blame me for her state of mind?"

Cory shrugged. "I always did think it was because of you."

The old man frowned and leaned forward. "Why on earth would she pine for me?"

Cory laughed softly. "She loved you. I'm not sure why,

but she did. She never said a word against you, even when I wanted to believe the worst."

"She never got married?"

"Never."

"Boyfriends?"

"One. She dated a guy named Hank. He didn't last, though. And there weren't any others after him."

"So you think she was waiting around for me?" Uncertainty entered the old man's quavering tone.

"Yeah, I do."

"No way." His father shook his head. "Love doesn't wait around for thirty years. Fear might. Resentment, perhaps. But not love."

"What makes you so sure?" Cory asked.

"I'm not worth the wait." He spread his hands on the table, then coughed and leaned his head back against his chair, seemingly tired.

"Do you need a rest?" Cory asked.

"Yes, but I think we need to talk about this." He heaved a wheezy sigh. "Far be it from me to speak ill of the dead, but have you considered that perhaps your mother might have had some emotional problems?"

Cory gave his father an angry glance. Emotional problems? He was going to try to call her unbalanced?

"She was perfectly stable," he replied coldly.

"But not happy."

Cory didn't answer. No, she hadn't been happy much of the time. She'd been tired from work, or frustrated over the finances. There was always an excuse, but Cory had blamed his father for leaving her the way he did. Had that been childish naïveté? Had she been suffering from depression, perhaps? It was funny how a child processed these things, and sometimes in adulthood a man forgot to adjust his assumptions.

"I don't want to upset you," his father said quietly. "I

know how a man feels about his mother. My mother was a saint, and you can't convince me otherwise. But sometimes things are more complicated than children realize.

"Look at me. Do I look like the kind of guy who could ruin a woman for all other men?" The old man shook his head. "Normally, people move on and love again. That kind of pining happens in movies, not real life."

Cory spooned some sugar into his mug. Did his father have a point?

"And look at you," his father said. "I'm pretty sure you've loved before, but you're considering another woman—" He laughed tiredly. "But you won't admit it and we can't talk about her, apparently."

Cory wasn't amused and gave the old man a tight smile, then sipped his tea. His father shifted in his chair, his breath coming in audible whispers.

"I can't take responsibility for your mother's unhappiness. For lying, cheating and being a general scoundrel, absolutely, but not for your mother's choices."

Why didn't she move on? Was she waiting for him to leave his wife?

That thought hurt because it didn't jibe with who he had believed his mother to be. She'd raised him in church, even when he'd fought against her. She'd insisted upon truthfulness and honesty. She told him that a good man was trustworthy, even in the little things. She accepted nothing less than the absolute best from him.

As the wind rose outside and the rain pattered against the glass, he wished he'd never delved into this—never asked any questions at all. He'd rather remember his mother on a pedestal than know the worst about both of his parents.

Eloise padded into the kitchen, a sweater around her shoulders. She wore a pair of blue jeans and a loose T-shirt, her feet bare. She glanced uneasily toward the window.

The DJ stopped his banter and Cory leaned over to turn up the volume. "A severe weather warning has been issued for Blaine County. Strong winds, rain, hail and lightning are expected. Prepare accordingly."

Cory pushed himself to his feet. He knew what that meant, and his work was just about to start in earnest. His mind revved forward to what they'd have to get done in the next couple of hours—bringing in the horses and cattle, separating the pregnant cows…the list went on. He wanted to get out there as soon as possible to give Zach a hand and get the ranch hands organized.

"Find the candles," he said, heading into the mudroom. "They're under the sink, and you'll probably need them. We always lose power in the big storms."

"Is everything okay?" Eloise asked, her face appearing around the corner of the mudroom.

"I've got to get the animals into the barn. We have some new calves, and they need shelter." He slammed his feet into his boots and grabbed an oiled raincoat. "And Eloise?"

"Hmm?" Worry flickered in her green eyes.

He dropped his hat on his head. "Stay put. These storms can get really bad."

He caught her gaze and held it, willing her to understand the dangers that he had no time to explain.

"Okay?" he said. "I'm serious. Stay put."

She nodded. With that, he pulled open the door and stepped out into the wind.

Eloise's stomach tightened as the rain pounded against the glass. A sick greenish color seeped through the clouds, and the wind shrieked past the house, as if it were moaning in agony. Mr. Bessler had already gone for a long sleep and had woken up again, but Cory had not returned.

"What's taking so long?" Mr. Bessler asked uneasily. "He's been gone this whole time, right?"

"This is a big ranch."

What did she know? She only meant to reassure her patient, and herself. The storm had whipped itself up into a frightening fury, rain lashing the house, wind howling around buildings and lightning cracking across the sky with heart-stopping thunder.

"I've never seen a storm last this long," Mr. Bessler murmured.

The lights flickered, then went out, sinking them into dusk-like darkness. Eloise heaved a sigh. Cory had warned them. A lightning bolt illuminated the room in a flash; then all was dim once more.

"Are you all right, Robert?" she asked.

"Fine, fine, I'm not a baby," the old man muttered.

Eloise pulled out the candles and opened the box of matches, but then a thought occurred to her.

"Do you need your oxygen? Lighting candles next to oxygen isn't a great idea, so—"

"No." His slippers swished against the floor as he rolled in her direction. "I'm fine. Go ahead."

Eloise lit two of the candles and carried them to the kitchen table. The flickering light pulled Eloise and Mr. Bessler toward the warm glow. A dribble of wax slid down the side of one, and Eloise leaned her head back, listening as the rain pelted the window panes. Outside, between crashes of thunder, a strange noise filtered through. Mr. Bessler shifted in his chair, and then she saw the urn in his hands.

"Robert, why do you have Ruth's ashes?" she asked.

"I—" He looked down at the urn. "I was going to remind you that I need to scatter them."

"I know." She nodded. "We'll be sure to do that."

Mr. Bessler put the urn on the table. Eloise had a feeling that he just missed Ruth and liked to have her close in whatever way he could. A sound caught her attention from outside, and she frowned.

"Did you hear that?" she asked.

"Hear what?"

Eloise paused again to listen but didn't hear anything past the howling wind.

"It's gone." She shrugged. "Are you hungry? Can I get you anything?"

The old man shook his head. "You're always trying to feed me."

"You need to keep your strength up."

"For what?" he asked sarcastically. "To grow up strong and healthy?"

Eloise rolled her eyes. "Everyone needs to eat."

The wind died down for just a moment, and Eloise heard the noise again, this time quite clearly.

"That!" she said. "Did you hear that?"

"It's a cow," Mr. Bessler replied. "A calf, actually."

Eloise rose to her feet and peered out the window, shading her eyes to see as far as she could into the murky downpour. The thin wail from the calf wound around the thunderclaps and patter of rain.

"Are you sure?" she asked uncertainly.

"Definitely. That's how they call their mothers."

"Poor thing…" Eloise looked back at her patient, who sat comfortably at the kitchen table, then turned toward the door, listening. "It must be terrified. There were some newborns today, you know. It might be one of them."

The calf bawled again, and Eloise went to the window and attempted to see through the rain. Her heart went out the calf, alone and afraid in the storm.

"Robert, I can't leave that animal out there."

"Cory told you stay put."

She remembered Cory's warning, and she looked back out the window.

"It can't be far if we can hear it."

"Then go get it," the old man said.

The thought had only half formed in her mind, but when Mr. Bessler said it so matter-of-factly, she wondered if she could. It was a baby and needed help—why not see?

"Will you be okay by yourself?"

"Where am I going to go?"

"I've got my cell phone on me, and—"

"I'm fine!"

Eloise smiled. "I'll be back in a few minutes. I won't be long, okay?"

She pushed her feet into a pair of old gum boots that looked as if they might be only a little too big, then tugged a rain jacket around her shoulders. Now was not the time for fashion. When she opened the door, a wall of rain drenched her. Shivering against the chill, she pushed outside and slammed the door solidly behind her. From her left, she heard the plaintive bawl.

"God, let me find it…" she prayed aloud.

The rain whipped around her, nearly blinding her, and she lifted an arm to shield her face. A tree limb tumbled down the road a few paces away, rolling end over end in the driving wind, and her heart skipped a beat.

Once more, the calf's cry came, this time weaker. Stumbling in the direction of the sound, she paused again, straining her eyes against the weather.

"Eloise!" a voice called, and she turned to see Cory's big form striding down the road toward her. His coat whipped around him and he broke into a jog.

"Cory!" she called. "Come here!"

The big man hurried up, breathing hard. "What happened? Is my dad all right? What are you doing out here?"

"Listen," she ordered, putting a hand on his arm. The sound came again, fainter still. "Do you hear that?"

"A calf," he said.

She nodded. "I could hear it inside the house. I was trying to find it."

"Well, go back inside. I'm here now."

"Let me help you." She angled her steps in the direction of the sound, ignoring the muttered irritation coming from Cory behind her.

"I can't carry both you and a calf," he retorted.

"Who says I need carrying?" she shot back. "Come on already!"

The wind pushed against her, nearly rocking her off her feet more than once, but she pressed on.

"This way!" Cory yelled into the wind, and Eloise turned her labored steps after him.

A smudge of brown huddled behind a bush, curled up in the wet grass, its chocolate-brown coat soaked with rain. Thunder crashed overhead and the calf ducked its head and bawled in fear.

"Hey there, little guy," Cory murmured, hunkering down low. "It's okay. Come here…"

The calf resisted Cory's attempt to lift it, and Cory muttered again under his breath. Eloise sank down next to the calf and stroked its wet head. It lay next to a broken fence, splinters of wood shooting out like claws. At least they knew how he got out here.

Cory looked at the broken fence and sighed. "It looks like we lost a few cows through here. Let's get him over to the barn."

The murky shape of the cow barn hunched in the distance, and she looked at the calf uncertainly. "Can we make it?" she asked.

"No choice."

A pair of headlights bounced down the road and slowed as the truck rumbled up to where they crouched. Nora rolled down the window.

"What's going on?" she shouted over the gale.

"A calf," Cory called back. "We need to get him back to the barn."

"Zack is there now—I was just going to pick him up," she hollered back. "Put the calf in the back, and I'll take him over."

Cory put a gloved hand under the calf's rump and another under the chest. He grunted as he rose to his feet. The calf wriggled in his arms, and Cory slipped, falling heavily against the broken fence rail. He grimaced and exhaled a huff of air. Overhead, lightning cracked and the calf lurched in his arms.

"Are you okay?" Eloise shouted over the boom of thunder.

He nodded and winced as he lifted the calf again. Getting his feet under him, Cory struggled to stand and headed toward the truck. As he hoisted the calf into the back of the vehicle, it scrambled to its feet, hooves skidding against the truck bed.

"He'll try to stand up and only hurt himself more. I'd better ride with him," Cory said, swinging his leg over the side and easing next to the calf.

The calf didn't calm down with Cory next to it. It kept pushing its blunt nose toward Eloise, hooves scrambling.

"Let me help," Eloise shouted above the wind.

He called back, "Come on. Get in."

He held out a hand. Eloise followed his example and swung her leg up. The truck was slick with mud and rain, and the cold metal chilled her leg through her jeans. Cory grabbed her arm and hauled her over the edge. Eloise settled down next to Cory's warm side, putting a reassuring hand on the calf's flank as she caught her breath. The calf leaned closer to her and lay down. She felt a thrill of pride that her presence made a difference for it. The truck lurched forward and crunched along the gravel road toward the barn, and Eloise rocked with the motion of the vehicle, her arm pressed against Cory's strong body.

"I wouldn't have found this one," Cory said, leaning his head down. "It's a good thing you heard it."

She grinned at him. "I earn my keep."

He caught her smile and laughed. "That you do."

Cory took his hat off and dropped it onto her head, shielding her face from the lashing rain. Rivulets of water dripped down his face, and he wiped them away with a swipe of his arm.

"I need to get back to your dad," Eloise said. "He was fine when I left him, but I don't like him to be alone in his condition."

Cory nodded, and as the truck slowed to a stop in front of the big building, he hopped out.

"Stay here," he said and hurried to the barn door. He disappeared for a moment, then reemerged with Zack on his heels. Zack and Cory eased the calf out of the truck; then Nora took over, helping her husband guide the frightened animal into the barn door—to warmth and safety.

Cory turned back to Eloise. "They'll take care of it from here," he said. "Come on. Let's get you back."

He held out a hand and steadied her as she climbed down from the truck, the loose boots making her steps awkward when she dropped to the muddy ground.

"Can you walk it?" he asked. "Zack will need the truck to go pick up some of the ranch hands who are working farther out."

"Of course." Her jeans, now streaked with mud, clung to her legs. She stumbled once and he shot out a hand, grabbing hers in his strong grip. He tugged her closer to him, his broad shoulder sheltering her from some of the stinging rain.

"Stay close," he ordered, his voice low and near, and she willingly obliged. Sheets of rain and mist veiled her view. They hurried along the muddy road, heads ducked, but his steely hand wrapped around hers brought her a rush of warm comfort.

"Almost there," Cory's voice rumbled into her ear. "This way."

Eloise's boot slid against some mud, her foot slipping sideways.

Oh, please let that be mud!

She clutched at Cory's arm to regain her balance and her fingers met with something sticky and warm. She knew the feel of blood, and there was lots of it.

"Cory, you're hurt!" she gasped.

Cory felt the back of his arm with his free hand and winced. "I thought I nicked it."

"That's more than a nick." Eloise couldn't see much in the falling rain, but she knew how much blood she felt under her fingers. "Let's get back to the house where I can take a look at that."

Cory didn't put up any protest, and they made their way together toward the flickering candlelight in the window of the ranch house. He might know cattle and ranches, but she knew how much a human body could withstand, and this arm needed medical attention.

Chapter Twelve

Cory winced as Eloise peeled back his shirt, easing the fabric away from the wound. He hadn't noticed the severity of the injury at the time. He'd been so focused on getting the calf to safety and Eloise to the shelter of the house that discovering his bloodied arm irritated him. The timing was miserable. He tossed his shirt into a wet heap on the kitchen floor while Eloise examined his arm, the first-aid kit next to her. Her cool fingers lingered on his shoulder and she made a soft tut of concern.

Outside the window, the storm raged on, and he glanced toward the silent radio. He moved, intending to flick it on, when her grip grew firm on his shoulder.

"Sit down," Eloise said.

"I was just going to—"

"Sit." Her tone grew stern and she shot him a no-nonsense look.

Cory complied and sank into a kitchen chair next to his father's wheelchair. She was generally soft-spoken, but when this woman gave an order, it was almost impossible to refuse. She crouched next to him, gently cleaning the blood away from the cut, and deposited the wet gauze pads beside him on the table.

"Bossy, isn't she?" the old man said, snickering.

"This is pretty deep, Cory." Eloise rose to her feet. "You can get away without stitches, but I'll have to clean it out." She opened the first-aid kit, and he couldn't see what she was up to behind him. Instead he looked over at his father, who watched the process with a slight grimace on his weathered face.

"What's she doing?" Cory asked.

"You'll find out soon enough," his father replied, and gave him a wicked smile.

"Bring those candles closer, would you?" she said.

Cory slid the candles toward them, gritting his teeth against the ache as she pressed gauze into the wound.

"That should do it," she said. "Now, this might sting a little."

Cory didn't answer. It wasn't stitches, so it couldn't be that bad.

"Are you ready?" she asked.

"Yeah, go ahead," he said, and he was met with a burning sensation so painful that he sucked in a breath past his teeth.

"Are you done?" he asked through gritted teeth.

"Once more," she replied cheerily. "Hold on…"

Again the burning pain seared into the wound. When it subsided, Cory turned around and glared at the bottle in her hand.

"What is that?" he demanded.

"Iodine," she replied. "Now sit still, would you?"

His father rasped out a laugh. "She's a mean one."

"Oh, hush," she replied in good humor. "Trust me, this is much less painful than an infected wound. The worst is over."

Eloise moved his arm away from his body, and he held still while she wrapped gauze around his biceps, layer after layer. She moved slowly, her cool touch lingering against his skin as she adjusted the bandage. When she taped down the bandage, he reached back to gingerly touch her handiwork.

"Now," Cory said, turning to face her. "About today—"

"You're very welcome." Eloise shot him a brilliant smile. "How does it feel?"

He looked down at his arm. "Pretty good. Thanks." She'd thrown him off his lecture. "About today, though—"

"You, um, should probably go find a shirt," she said quietly.

He glanced toward his father, who shrugged. "Downright indecent," the old man quipped. "Might as well go put something on."

Muttering irritably, Cory pushed himself off the chair. The house was still swathed in darkness, and he grabbed a candle from the table and headed out of the kitchen to his bedroom. He put the candle on his dresser before opening a drawer.

In his head, he was still mentally lecturing Eloise about the dangers of storms and ranches while he pulled out a white T-shirt and eased it over his wounded arm.

From the kitchen an enraged wail echoed through the house. Without another thought, Cory sprinted in the direction of the shout.

Eloise stared down in horror. The urn lay on its side, the ashes spread over the floor in a dusty spray.

"What have you done?" the old man shouted.

"Robert, I'm so sorry," Eloise said. "I didn't see it. I turned and—" She crouched down, attempting to scoop the ashes back into the container.

"Don't touch her." Mr. Bessler trembled in rage.

"What do you want me to do?" she asked, sitting back on her heels. "I'm so sorry," she repeated. "I didn't mean to."

"Of course not," the old man spat. "You never do, do you?"

Eloise stared at her patient in surprise. "What are you talking about?"

"One thing matters to me. One! And that is to scatter my wife's ashes."

"Robert, I didn't—"

"Ruth deserves respect. How did you ever become a nurse being so clumsy?"

Mr. Bessler's words stung, but she knew that they were rooted in fear. He wanted to scatter Ruth's ashes, and his own mortality was looming large. She took a deep breath, refusing to fuel her patient any further.

"What happened?" a voice rumbled, and Eloise looked up to see Cory's broad shoulders filling the doorway.

"That clumsy woman—"

"Watch it." There was warning in Cory's tone.

"I still pay you," Mr. Bessler muttered, glowering in Eloise's direction.

"You should be grateful she stays," Cory retorted. "If it weren't for Eloise, you'd be at home alone. From what I can tell, you don't have many people who care whether you live or die."

"Maybe I like it that way." The old man's eyes flashed fire.

"And maybe you're just a cranky old man who chases away everyone who cares about him." Cory shrugged.

Mr. Bessler narrowed his eyes and lifted a knobby finger. "You have no right to judge me."

"Maybe not." Cory squatted down next to Eloise and cupped a hand, carefully scooping the ashes together into a pile. "But here's the thing." He moved slowly, carefully, his tone low and controlled. "I don't like you talking to Eloise that way. She hasn't done anything to deserve you berating her like that."

"Do you see what she did?" the old man asked.

"An accident, yes. But I'll tell you this—while no one

else in your life seems to care about you, this woman does."
He lifted his gaze to meet the angry eyes of his father.
"She thinks about your needs constantly. She has made
your comfort her life's work."

"A job," the old man muttered.

"She *likes* you." Cory caught the old man's gaze and
held it. "You can't pay someone to do that. She stands up
for you. She points out the good in you."

Mr. Bessler sank into silence, and Cory continued
scooping the ash back into the urn with careful, measured
movements.

"I don't know why you think it's all right to treat people like this, but Eloise deserves better from you. Whether
you want to know me or not, I care how you treat Eloise."

The old man remained silent.

"While you're under my roof, you'll treat her with the
respect a lady is due."

"She's no lady, she's my nurse," he attempted to joke.
This was normally how Mr. Bessler's bad temper ended,
but his son didn't seem to know the cues.

"She's every inch a lady." Cory's voice rang out low
and direct.

Silence settled over the room, and the old man shuffled
his slippers uncomfortably.

"Fine." Mr. Bessler looked away, his jaw set.

Cory set the urn back on the table, then looked at Eloise.
"Are you okay?"

"Yes, I'm fine," she replied.

"I've got to go check on the herd. I'll be back in a while."

He'd only just gotten back to the house, and Eloise
suspected he was making an excuse to get out of there
again. The electricity flickered, then blazed on and Eloise squinted in the sudden light. Cory stood before her
with hands balled up into frustrated fists, and her patient
hunched irritably into his wheelchair.

"No problem," Eloise said.

"I'll see you both in a couple of hours."

As Cory headed to the mudroom and pulled on a rain jacket, Eloise mutely met her patient's gaze. He gave her an apologetic shrug.

"Sorry I yelled," the old man muttered.

"It's okay."

The door banged shut as Cory left. The house felt emptier without him in it. Eloise felt mildly stunned. Mr. Bessler's moodiness was par for the course, but Cory had just defended her honor, demanded that her patient treat her kindly, and then stomped out the door. She'd never had a man get that worked up about how she was treated, and the realization warmed her. She felt oddly protected, although she didn't need the protection. She had been well in control of the situation.

That was downright sweet, she admitted.

"So you stand up for me, do you?" her patient inquired.

"Of course," Eloise replied. "That's what friends do for each other."

The old man looked down. "Well, thank you."

She nodded.

"Ruth was like that. She always did see something in me worth keeping."

Eloise pulled her hair away from her face. "I'm sorry I spilled Ruth."

"I've dumped her out twenty times by now." Mr. Bessler batted his hand through the air. "She used to be twice as full as this."

Eloise smothered a grin. "Now that we've got some electricity, let's get some supper on. What do you want to eat?"

Chapter Thirteen

The next morning, the sun peeked over the horizon, flooding the fields in pink. The storm from the day before had left a streak of clouds in its wake, white tufts tinged with fuchsia as the sun edged higher. The morning hung in dew-drenched stillness, only the twitter of birds breaking the silence. Eloise sat on a bench on the veranda, a sketchpad on her lap, but her mind wasn't on her drawing this morning.

A breeze carrying the scent of fresh rain played through her curls and she wrapped her arms around herself. Mornings like this one with perfect quiet made her feel closer to God.

Her heart stretched toward her Maker with a wordless prayer. Everything seemed possible at sunrise, before her misgivings had a chance to take hold. In the early morning, Eloise felt clean and brand-new.

A swarm of sparrows danced through the sky in a choreographed ball of fluttering wings, rising up from a bunch of trees, the whole group swaying one way, then another as they moved on in search of food.

She couldn't help remembering the sparrows of the Bible:

Are not two sparrows sold for a farthing? and one of them shall not fall on the ground without your Father...

Fear ye not therefore, ye are of more value than many sparrows.

The birds rose again and moved like drops of water-color, slipping across the sky, a vast form of fluttering life. A feeling of peace swept over her. Her life had been turned upside down over the past couple of years, but she wasn't out of His hand.

Behind Eloise, the front door opened and she turned. Cory stood in the doorway in jeans and a white T-shirt, his feet bare. He held two steaming mugs.

"Am I disturbing you?" he asked.

"Not if that's coffee," she said with a grin.

He stepped outside and handed her a mug. "Mind if I join you?"

Eloise scooted over to give him space, and he sank onto the bench next to her, his arm touching hers. He rested his elbows on his knees, his coffee cup dwarfed between his broad palms.

"I love dawn," she said softly. "Your dad won't wake up for another couple of hours, and this is time I get to myself."

"I am intruding, aren't I?" His dark gaze met hers, and a smile curved one side of his mouth.

"No." She chuckled. "It's okay. I can share dawn with you."

"I like sunrises, too," Cory said. "It's a quiet time before the work starts." He nodded to the pad of paper in her lap. "Writing?"

"Drawing. It's relaxing."

"What are you drawing this morning?"

Eloise briefly considered keeping her work private, then dismissed it. She opened the pad to her most recent page, the sketches still rough, but getting closer to her intention.

"May I?" Cory asked, and when she nodded, he took the

pages from her hands and looked at them more closely. He looked over at her, respect in his eyes. "It's me."

Eloise looked down. "I told you I wanted to draw your eyes."

"I know." His tone was soft and he turned his attention back to the page. "The lines around my eyes, this scar on my eyebrow…"

She nodded. "I'm flattered that you recognized yourself."

"You're really good."

"It's just a hobby."

He shook his head. "No, it's more than that."

"An outlet."

"That's probably closer to the truth." Cory looked at the page thoughtfully. "My eyes—is this what you see?"

"I think about your hands, too," Eloise replied. "I wanted to try your eyes because they say so much. If I could capture any part of you, I thought it would be your eyes."

A playful smile teased the corners of his lips. "I could say something cheesy about you being able to capture my heart."

Eloise laughed out loud.

"So, what about the rest of the ranch? Does it make you want to paint?"

"It does." She paused, then laughed softly. "I have to admit, I've been out of my element here. It's a bit embarrassing."

"You're not that bad."

She shot him an incredulous look. "Liar. But I appreciate the effort." She let her eyes roam over the pastoral scene before her. "But this morning, looking out on all of this, I see something different. It's more than beautiful, it's—" she cast about looking for a way to describe the hopeful lift in her heart "—closer to God, somehow."

"I feel that way, too." He took a sip of coffee. "When I was a kid, I used to come out here and look out on this same scene during the summers. It was different then. More seemed possible." He glanced at her uncertainly. "Do you know what I mean?"

She nodded. "I get it."

"I used to think about what my life would be when I grew up. I wanted a horse and a wife. In that order."

Eloise grinned. "You had your priorities."

He smiled. "I was twelve. Maybe thirteen. The horse really did seem more important then."

"And a wife?" she asked. "What kind of wife did you want?"

"A pretty one, who could fix a car."

She tipped her head to the side. "A tall order, but you could probably find her."

"I've changed my mind about the mechanic part." Cory chuckled. "What about you? What kind of guy did you dream about marrying when you were a kid?"

"I wanted to marry a man who wore a suit to work and brought home flowers." Her mind went back to her girlhood fantasies. "Philip did those things. It wasn't enough."

"So how flexible are you about that suit?" he asked, teasing in his eye.

"I could live without it."

Silence stretched between them, the warmth of his arm next to hers so comforting that Eloise leaned against him, enjoying his strength. Cory shifted his weight and slid his arm around her, pulling her against his side.

Dare she get used to this—a handsome guy bringing her coffee and holding her close?

"I have to say, you surprised me yesterday."

"Oh?" She glanced up at him.

"I never expected you to go out after a calf."

"I couldn't very well leave it out there."

Cory nodded slowly. "You've got some country in you after all."

Eloise laughed softly. "I'm not some little weakling, you know."

"Didn't say you were."

"But you were thinking it." She glanced up teasingly.

He shrugged. "Maybe. But you've proven me wrong, that's for sure. Now if I could just get you back on a horse."

"Not going to happen," Eloise responded. "How's your arm?"

"It's fine."

"Sore?" she asked.

"Not that I'll admit to."

Eloise shook her head. "I've reconsidered since last night. I think it might need stitches."

"It'll be fine."

"The scar will be worse without them," she warned.

He laughed, the sound low and warm. "Since when do I look afraid of a few scars?"

"We're all afraid of scars," she replied softly.

"Are you?"

Eloise nodded slowly. "Definitely."

Cory picked up the pad of drawing paper once more and flipped through the pages. The silence was peppered with the morning calls of birds.

"You're tougher than you think, Eloise."

"What makes you so sure?"

"You stayed on the back of a runaway horse. You plowed through a storm to find a calf. You take care of my ornery old father every single day."

"Tough, maybe," she agreed. "But strength is something different."

"How so?" He shifted to face her and brushed a curl away from her cheek with the back of a finger.

"Strength is more graceful," she said. "It's more beautiful. Toughness is filled with scars and desperation."

"I beg to differ." Cory's voice stayed low and he brushed his finger over her cheek again, his dark gaze enveloping hers. "You're gorgeous."

Eloise laughed softly and dropped her gaze to the drawing pad in her lap. "You're a sweet talker."

"I'm honest."

Eloise pushed herself forward to stand up. "I should probably—"

Cory leaned forward at the same time, and they both froze, their faces only a whisper apart. She swallowed, her breath catching in her throat. His warm breath tickled her face.

"I should probably..." she murmured again.

"Yeah." He didn't move away, though. "Me, too."

"I..." She stopped trying to articulate anything and hesitantly looked into his dark, gentle eyes. Then his lips came down onto hers, and her eyes fluttered shut. For a moment, everything but the two of them seemed to evaporate, and Eloise felt a deep longing inside.

She wanted *this*. She wanted love and passion, kisses as the sun rose, basking together in the pink clouds of a new day. She wanted to be held, to have someone think about her during the day—she wanted all of it. When Cory pulled back, she blinked open her eyes to find him looking down into her face, a smile on his lips.

As Eloise looked into his ruggedly handsome face, the morning stubble on his chin and the lines around his eyes, she suddenly felt a flare of uncertainty. She swallowed hard and looked away, struggling to control her emotions.

"Are you okay?" Cory asked, worry edging his tone.

"This is exactly what I want, but I'm still afraid to trust someone," she admitted.

"I'm not like your ex, you know," he said quietly. "I wouldn't hurt you."

She shook her head sadly. "I didn't think he would, either."

Cory eased away from her, giving her space. "Okay."

"Are we still friends?" she asked tentatively.

"Of course." He rose to his feet and met her gaze for a long moment as if he were contemplating something, then stepped toward the front door of the house. His broad shoulders blocked out the rising sun behind him so that he showed a tall, muscular silhouette. "I'd better get to work."

She nodded.

"Hey."

She met his gaze again and he said, "I meant it. I'm not."

Cory didn't wait for her to answer but opened the door and stepped inside, leaving her alone in the cool morning breeze that smelled of rain, grass and moist earth.

Cory tossed a coil of rope into the back of his pickup and hopped into the driver's seat.

"What was I thinking?" he muttered angrily to himself. "Lord, I'm failing at this—"

He slammed the truck into first gear and pulled out onto the twisting gravel road. He was absolutely blowing it. He was supposed to be keeping his distance, so what was he doing kissing her? Since when was that part of the plan?

But he had to admit that it felt amazing. She'd been so close, so open and sweet…

"Doesn't matter. She's not mine to kiss."

Truth be told, he was lonely. He'd buried his desire for a wife when Deirdre walked out on him, but lately, Eloise had awakened those old longings for a woman in his life, a wife with whom he could share this land.

She doesn't want this any more than Deirdre did, he reminded himself. His truck rounded the corner to Zack and

Nora's little house where Zack stood on the porch, waiting for him. He passed his coffee mug to Nora and leaned over to give her kiss.

"You're late!" Zack called good-naturedly.

"I know. Sorry."

Zack walked over and pulled open the passenger-side door. "Nice morning, isn't it?"

"Yeah."

He stepped on the gas and they eased back onto the gravel road that led toward the barn.

"So how are you liking having a woman in the house?" Zack teased.

Cory shot his friend an irritated glare. He might be getting hung up on a pretty redhead, but it was the same story all over again—Cory Stone falling for the woman who wanted the opposite of everything he had to offer.

"Whoa. Sorry, man. Just joking around." Zack put his hands up.

"I'm not in the mood," Cory said.

"Why not? What happened?"

Cory eased to a stop in front of the barn and turned off the engine. "I kissed her."

"Really, now." Zack's eyebrows shot up. "This sounds like a good thing."

"Nope, it was a stupid thing," Cory replied, pushing open the door and hopping out.

"Why?" Zack demanded, slamming his door shut and following Cory to the barn door.

Cory tipped his hat back on his head and slapped his gloves irritably across his thigh. "Because now I want to do it again."

Chapter Fourteen

"Are you ready to sleep, Robert?" Eloise asked cheerfully, closing the curtains against the sunlight. She'd just cleaned up the last of their dishes from lunch, and her patient was quickly wilting.

"I could sleep." His voice was weak.

Eloise took out his medication chart and checked her watch. As she put his pills into a paper cup, the old man heaved a sigh.

"I need to scatter Ruth."

"I know." She opened the last pill bottle and double-checked the dosage.

"Red..." His voice was soft, rousing Eloise from the pills.

"Yes, Robert?"

"I mean it. It needs to happen. Soon."

Eloise sank down to the bed beside him. "I'll talk to your son."

He nodded weakly. "I might not have been good to anyone else in my life, but I want to do right by Ruth."

"Sir, you've done right by me," Eloise said softly.

"Have I?" He looked doubtful.

She nodded. "You give me hope."

"For what?"

"For the kind of love you had with Ruth. My marriage fell apart, but you two had something that was stronger. You had your struggles, but you made it. That's the goal, isn't it?"

The old man sighed. "Well, I'll have a lot of explaining to do when I get to heaven, I imagine."

"Let me talk to Cory. As soon as he comes back, I'll bring it up. I promise."

Mr. Bessler nodded and reached toward the urn on the bedside table. Eloise put it in his hands, and his bony fingers wrapped around the metal container. He closed his eyes and heaved a sigh.

He's close to the end.

She knew by instinct, and she blinked back a mist of tears.

If nothing else, Mr. Bessler was a prime example of a man in love, even after death had parted him from his wife. That was something extraordinary.

That evening, after a long day out in the fields, Cory came back in, his muscles aching. He'd been avoiding the house today, mostly out of embarrassment. By kissing Eloise, he had crossed a line, big-time.

He stood at the counter and put together a sandwich, then stayed there to eat it, not bothering to move to the table. It tasted better than Cory thought it would, and he took big, jaw-cracking bites, fresh bread and meat mingling with the tang of condiments. He bit into a crisp pickle and chewed thoughtfully.

Help me to settle this honorably, Father. I don't want to be that guy.

Finishing the sandwich, he put the plate in the sink.

"I'd better go do this," he muttered. Putting it off would only make things worse.

Heading down the hallway, he stopped at the library

door. Light shone warmly from within, and when he tapped lightly on the door, Eloise's soft voice called, "Come in."

Cory pushed open the door. Eloise sat in a leather chair, a book open in her lap. She smiled across the room at him, her green eyes glittering in the lamplight.

"Hi," he said sheepishly, stepping into the room. "How was your day?"

"Not bad," she said. "I promised your father, though, that I'd set a time to scatter his wife's ashes."

"Of course." Cory cleared his throat. "We can do it in the morning."

"He'll be relieved. It's the last thing he wants to do before—" She stopped, winced.

He walked farther into the room. "I actually wanted to apologize to you."

"For what?"

"That kiss."

Eloise's cheeks turned pink, and she looked away.

"I shouldn't have kissed you." His voice stayed low. "It wasn't your fault. It was all me."

"No, no," she replied, shutting the book and putting it aside. "It's just complicated—we should probably be careful, feeling the way we do."

That was the first time Eloise had mentioned feeling anything for him, and he found a spark of hope igniting deep inside.

"How do we feel?" Cory asked, his dark gaze meeting hers.

"Attracted to each other?" She arched an eyebrow elegantly. "That kiss wasn't just you, Cory. I take responsibility, too."

He felt the heat rising in his own face, and he chuckled softly. "Okay. So we're both feeling something."

"Let's just be careful," she repeated. "Maybe less time alone together would be good for us, and if we are alone, let's try to keep things—" she cleared her throat "—friendly. Nothing more."

"Agreed."

Eloise nodded, as if that resolved the issue, and he heaved a tired sigh.

"It's been a long day," Cory said. "Maybe I'll just grab a book and head off to bed."

He strode over to the bookshelf and scanned the titles for something relaxing. At the end of a row, he noticed a narrow tin box slipped in at the end of the books. It was the size of a hard-cover novel, so it didn't stand out.

That's weird, he thought, and tugged it free and tried the latch. It was obvious the tin hadn't been opened in a long time—it was difficult to open. He pried off the lid and pulled out a bundle of envelopes, yellowed with age, and frowned.

"What did you find?" Eloise asked.

"Letters, it looks like." He turned them over in his big hands.

"Whose?"

Cory looked at the address on the front of each envelope. "They're written to my mother."

He opened one and pulled out a single page of writing. He read silently, then put it aside, pulled out a second letter and read it through before looking down at Eloise quizzically.

"Who wrote them?"

"Robert."

Cory's heart hammered in his throat as he scanned the slanted handwriting:

Dear Shelley,
I know it's been a long time since I've written you,
but I've been thinking of you often. I can't help won-
dering if you're married yet, settling into that life I

*never could give you. What we had was so short, so
fleeting, that I don't understand why I still see you
in my dreams. But I do.*

*How is our son? He'd be five now, I believe. I
see other five-year-old children and it reminds me
of him. Of course, I can't tell Ruth about him, so I
sit alone and I'm swarmed by memories of you and
wishes for what could have been if I'd only been
stronger.*

*I'm enclosing a small amount of money for our
boy. It isn't much, but I can't take out more money
without my wife noticing. You know how these things
are with bitter women. Or maybe you don't.*

Write me, my love. I miss you.
Robert

Had his father really thought about him and sent money?
Ruth didn't sound like the lovely woman his father had
been talking about. It was strange to see him describing
his wife in this light. He flipped to the next letter.

Dear Shelley,
*I was so happy to get your letter. I know it's been a
few months, and I'm sorry for that. You said I'm married and that should count for something, and maybe
it does. But I'll tell you this—a marriage isn't always
as it appears. I wish you could trust me on this.*

*You asked how I am. I'm frustrated. I'm lonely.
I think of you too often, and I know that I'm a terrible father. I have no idea what Cory must think of
me. Don't let him hate me. Even if you hate me just
a little, protect me in his eyes. One day, I'll make it
up to him, I swear.*

*You asked if I might be able to visit you one of
these days, and I'm not sure I could make that hap-*

pen. *You know how jealous and controlling my wife is. I couldn't get away without her nagging me about it, and I don't dare tell her about you. It's for your own protection. There is no telling what she'd do.*

But enough about her. What about you? Are you seeing anyone? Does anyone else get to whisper sweet nothings into your ear? Don't tell me if you have someone. It would hurt to hear it, and I'd rather remember you as mine, and not have to face the reality of you moving on with someone else.

I'll write when I can. I'm enclosing a small amount of money. I'll send more next time, but maybe you could get something pretty for yourself.
With love,
Robert

Cory realized belatedly that Eloise had been reading over his shoulder, but he didn't mind. It saved him explanations.

"So they stayed in contact," Eloise said weakly.

"My dad told me that he had no idea why my mother might have held on to hope that they'd get back together." Cory heard the growl in his own tone. "He questioned her mental stability. He suggested that perhaps she had some emotional problems to make her react the way she did."

"How many letters are there?"

"Twenty? Thirty?" He looked down at the bundle in his hands and flipped through the first few. "They seem to be dated every six or eight months, and the ones I've read so far seem to be asking her to wait. Not openly, but between the lines."

"Did he love her, after all?" Eloise asked.

"He claimed to."

Cory rose to his feet, slapping the bundle against his

open palm. He opened another and read it through, his expression grim.

"So this means that your father had been writing love letters to your mother for years. He lied to Ruth for years…" Eloise shook her head slowly.

Cory folded the letter and returned it to the envelope.

"Are you all right?" Eloise asked, putting a hand on his arm.

"I'm fine." He nodded slowly, capping the anger that simmered in his middle.

"You're angry."

"Yes." Cory kept his voice low. His father was more manipulative than he'd ever imagined, and the realization slapped him in the gut.

"He's going to face God soon enough," she said softly. "He doesn't need our judgment, too."

Cory looked at the letters in his hand. "Does lying come that easily to him?" He shook his head. "Because I believed him. That's what gets me. I'm a pretty good judge of people, and when he told me that he had no idea why my mother might have pined for him, I actually believed it."

Eloise didn't answer, but compassion swam in those deep green eyes.

"It's late," he said gruffly. "I'm going to read the rest of these alone."

"Okay," she said, giving a faint nod. "We'll take your father out in the morning, then?"

He nodded curtly. "Sure. See you then."

Cory headed out of the library and down the hallway toward his bedroom. So much for restful reading—his emotions were reeling, and he needed some space to sort it out.

What had been happening between his parents all those years?

Chapter Fifteen

The next morning, the pickup sped down the highway, power lines looping along beside them. Fields stretched out on either side of the highway, rolling lazily toward the horizon. Grazing cattle dotted the lush green grass, trees springing up around the creeks that watered the land. A cloudless sky domed overhead, washing the landscape in sunlight. The day was beautifully hot, a perfect summer morning, but a heavy feeling enveloped Eloise as she regarded the pastoral scene outside the truck window.

She looked uneasily at her patient in the backseat. Mr. Bessler scowled, and when he sensed her scrutiny, his gaze flickered toward her.

"What?" the old man demanded.

"Are you feeling all right?" she asked. "Are you in pain?"

"I'm always in pain. The pills don't help anymore."

"I could ask your doctor to raise your dosage—"

"Leave me alone."

Eloise sighed and turned to face the front again. She was doing her best with the old man, but her feelings had changed when she read those letters. Mr. Bessler didn't have a short-lived fling and then regret it for the rest of his life; he'd had a fling and then written love letters to his mistress for years after the affair. How could a man claim to love his wife when he was writing those kinds of letters behind her back? For all of her curiosity about the secret to their long marriage, Eloise felt her admiration for Mr. Bessler's love shrivel. So this was what a lifelong marriage looked like—lies and emotional distances?

Anger simmered inside her, and she pressed it down.

Father, I need Your peace. Calm me. Help me not to take out my anger on a dying old man. Help me not to judge.

"Something's changed," Mr. Bessler said.

Eloise turned back. "What do you mean?"

"The two of you. Something's different."

Eloise and Cory glanced at each other.

Eloise shook her head. "I don't think so, Robert."

"I'm not stupid, I'm dying. Those are two different things." The old man shook his head irritably. "Now, what's going on?"

Tension rippled down Cory's jaw, and he pinned his eyes on the road ahead. For a couple of minutes no one spoke, some tinny banjo music from a country station filling the silence. Then Cory flicked off the radio.

"I found some letters," he said, his voice low. "Letters you wrote to my mother."

Mr. Bessler didn't reply.

"There is a whole stack of them. You wrote her a lot."

"*Not* a lot."

"Thirty-some letters," Cory retorted. "You told her that you loved her. You said you missed her. You said Ruth was a shrew, controlling, vindictive—"

"Stop it!" Mr. Bessler's voice rang through the truck. "Never mind what I said about Ruth. It didn't mean anything."

"How could it not?" Cory asked, his voice rising. "Robert, you wrote Mom again and again, telling her how miserable you were with your wife!"

"Maybe I did, but how often?" The old man's voice quavered. "How often? Tell me!"

"About twice a year."

"Exactly. That was how often Ruth and I would lock horns over some stupid thing. We'd fight and I'd have to apologize. That's how it works in a marriage—the man comes with cap in hand. Well, I didn't like it, and I got my revenge: I wrote a letter to my old mistress. Ruth was none the wiser."

"You made Ruth out to be a monster and claimed to still love my mother. What was Mom supposed to think?"

"They were harmless letters. I complained about my wife and remembered a woman I'd cared about. I never acted on them."

"Harmless?" Cory answered. "They kept my mother on a string all those years. Every time she might have been ready to move on with her life, she got another letter." His voice dripped disgust. "You said that my mother must have had emotional problems, but that wasn't the case at all, was it?"

A semi truck lumbered past, the wake of wind pushing against the pickup. Cory didn't take his eyes off the road, but his expression remained grim.

Mr. Bessler's eyes flashed in fury. "Even if I'd promised the moon, why should she have believed me? I never called. I never visited, and all those years, I never once left my wife. I never intended to. Yes, I lied and lied and lied. You can judge me for being a terrible husband if you want. I was a terrible father, too, but you can't blame it on me when a woman decides to put her life on hold for a few honeyed words. Anyone who believes words over actions needs their head examined."

Mr. Bessler's rage was spent and he leaned his head back, breathing deeply from his oxygen mask. Cory stared with flinty directness at the road ahead.

"Is this still your land, boy?" the old man asked after a moment.

"We're just passing it now," Cory replied.

"Find me a place to scatter Ruth, then."

Cory complied, pulling off the highway onto a side road that made the truck rattle and bump as they drove along. At a small bridge, Cory eased the truck to a stop. Far behind them, an odd car or truck would speed past on the highway, but on this particular road, all was deserted.

"My land is that way," Cory said, gesturing to the right. "But everything over this way belongs to another ranch. Will this do?"

A wooden bridge spanned a babbling creek. Tall trees rose along the banks, the sunlight filtering through the leaves and scattering shadows over the planks of wood. A few round, wet stones rose up in the creek below and water gurgled around them. Beyond the trees that lined the bank, fields rolled out on either side, cloud shadows slinking along the rippling surface of the crops.

"It'll do fine," Mr. Bessler pronounced.

Cory lifted out the wheelchair and Eloise settled the old man into it, his wife's urn in his trembling grasp. She released his brakes and slowly wheeled him onto the bridge.

"Is this spot all right?" she asked.

"Point me that way." He flicked a hand in the direction of the other rancher's property. Eloise adjusted his chair and set the brake.

"I'll give you some privacy," she said quietly.

Eloise walked back to the truck where Cory waited. A breeze cooled her back and she paused, her gaze roaming over the wide, prairie sky. Wisps of white stretched across the blue, growing misty along the horizon. She leaned against the grill of the truck next to Cory.

"It's not half so romantic when you know the details, is it?" Cory asked softly.

"It certainly loses something," she agreed.

"I can't believe my mom hung her hopes on him." Cory's jaw was tense.

"I hung my hopes on Philip. It happens."

Cory scraped his boot against the gravel. "It's not that she made a mistake with my father. I can forgive that easily enough. It's that she never moved on from it."

Eloise shrugged. "There are no easy answers, are there?"

"Never seem to be."

The gentle breeze and gurgle of the creek lulled them into a companionable silence. Mr. Bessler hunched in his wheelchair. He stared down at the urn, his white hair shifting in the light breeze.

Eloise could only guess at Cory's emotions. She reached over and put a hand on his arm, his muscles rippling under her touch. He glanced down at her, his dark eyes meeting hers.

On the bridge, Mr. Bessler pried open the lid to the urn. With a few murmured words that did not carry, he leaned forward and poured the contents over the edge of the bridge. The ashes tumbled over each other, billowing out in a soft breath of gray as they met the puffs of breeze.

"Rest in peace," Cory murmured.

Just as the ashes fell free of the urn, a gust of wind rose, caught them and whisked them in the other direction. It happened so quickly that Mr. Bessler didn't seem to notice at first. His expression remained grim and forlorn, but when he saw the direction the ashes moved, his eyes widened in horror.

Eloise stared in mute surprise as the ashes blew straight back to Cory's property.

"Oh no," she whispered, but her words were drowned out by the shout of fury that erupted from the frail old man.

He flung down the urn, which bounced twice, clanging against the bridge deck.

Eloise propelled herself forward, afraid he'd hurt himself, but when she arrived at his side, he glared up at her, his lips trembling.

"She does not belong with *him*."

"She's not with Cory," Eloise replied. "She's with God."

"Thirty-five years," he said, his voice a quivering whisper. "Thirty-five years and I still can't get it right."

"Robert, her remains are going back to the earth. Does it matter what side of a property line they fall on?"

"Yes!" The old man glared in the direction her ashes had flown. "And she would have enjoyed that."

"Why?" Cory's deep voice broke into their conversation. "Why would she enjoy it?"

"Because like you, Ruth always knew exactly who to blame." He shook his head dismally. "If she'd known about my affair, she wouldn't have blamed a child."

"No one is blaming you right now, Robert," Eloise said.

"Aren't you?" His watery eyes moved between Eloise and Cory. "Of course you are."

He silently accepted the empty urn from Eloise and sank back into his chair. Eloise turned him around and pushed his chair over the wooden bridge, back toward the truck.

Cory remained silent as he walked with them. He pulled open the back door, ready to help lift the old man.

"I'm sorry," Mr. Bessler said, his red-rimmed gaze meeting Cory's.

"It's okay."

"I wasn't a good man. I tried to make up for it at the end, but I didn't."

Cory didn't answer, emotions battling in his features. He bent to help Eloise lift the old man, but as he did, Mr. Bessler put a knobby hand on his shoulder.

"Your mother should have moved on, and I'm sorry I held her back. I wasn't worth the sacrifice. She would have made someone a beautiful wife."

Tears misted Cory's eyes and he gave a curt nod. The old man seemed satisfied, and they settled him into the backseat of the truck. Leaning his head back, Mr. Bessler took a deep breath and shut his eyes.

The moon hung heavily over the fields that night. Cory stood in the kitchen, arms crossed over his chest. Outside, a cricket chirped a lonesome sonata, the sound filtering through the open window above the sink.

My father is a broken man.

Somehow that thought had never occurred to him in all his years of wondering about Robert Bessler. Superhero, CIA, spy, wealthy businessman…but never did Cory imagine his father was in pain. Resentment gave way to pity as he thought about the life his father had led. A lying man probably spent his life looking over his shoulder, waiting to be found out. To never be discovered seemed like a greater punishment in a man's life—no release from the burden, no relief from the guilt.

A creak on the floorboards roused Cory from his thoughts and he turned to find Eloise standing in the doorway. Her eyes were puffy and she pulled a hand through her hair, tugging the curls away from her face.

Cory nodded. "He's not doing so well, is he?"

"No." She sighed. "I need to take him back to Haggerston, to his own bed and house."

"Okay." Cory cleared his throat. "Have I made things worse?"

"No." Eloise shook her head. "He chose to come here, and he deserved an honest discussion as much as anyone else."

"When do you want to go back?" Cory asked hesitantly.

"Can you drive us in the morning?"

"Sure, if that's what you want." As for Cory, he didn't want to take her back. He wanted to keep her here with him indefinitely, even though he knew that was impossible. If he was going to tell her how he felt, it was now or never. He cleared his throat.

"Eloise, you said before that you felt something for me."

She dropped her gaze. "It's not as simple as that."

"Yeah, for me, too." He stepped closer. "I know you haven't been here long, but—" He cast about for the right words. How was he supposed to describe that feeling of coming back to the house, the warmth of the lights and the anticipation of seeing her? "I don't know how to say this, but it's been different with you here."

"That's sweet." She chuckled softly. "I feel a little underfoot."

"No... Okay, sometimes, but not after you figured things out a bit." He grinned. "Why don't you stay on as our medic?"

"Because I have to take your father home." Eloise met his gaze evenly. "You know that. I'm his nurse."

"What if I held the space for you for after my dad—" Cory frowned. It felt wrong to be making plans for after his father's death. "If you like it here, and you feel inspired to paint here, and enjoy the work—I sure could use a competent medic like you."

"No." Tears rose in Eloise's eyes and she shook her head. "I can't."

"Why not?" Cory pressed. "Are you really willing to just drop all of this, forget about it? About me?"

"So, do you want me to be the medic, or something more?" she asked.

"Something more," he admitted. "I'm crazy about you."

"If you'd asked me a few days ago, I might have answered differently," Eloise replied, her voice low. "Yes, I feel it, and I haven't felt like this for such a long time, but—"

Those words buoyed him up.

"That's got to be worth something," Cory said.

"It is!" She dashed a curl away from her forehead. "And getting to know your father, I was starting to believe in love and marriage again. I thought that maybe your father's marriage was an example of love conquering all."

Cory's stomach sank. His father wasn't a shining example of husbandly excellence. He was a disappointment in pretty much every relationship in his life, as far as he could see.

"I'm not Robert Bessler," he said woodenly.

"No, but I've been married before," Eloise replied. "And I thought that maybe your father held some kind of marital secret. He went back to his wife, instead of moving on with the other woman. That's pretty amazing. After Philip dumped me, I really wanted to know how to be that woman."

"Philip had the problem, not you," Cory responded.

"How do I know?" Something between irritation and passion sparkled in her green eyes. "I have no idea!"

"If only you could see yourself the way I see you." He smiled. "You're gorgeous, intelligent, strangely wise… I don't know how Philip ever tore his eyes off you."

Tears swam in her eyes. "You don't know me well enough."

"I know you better than you think." Cory closed the gap between them and ran a hand down her silky arm. She shook her head and stepped back, out of his reach.

"Cory, I can't live through more heartbreak."

"Preaching to the choir," he retorted. "Eloise, I agree— my father was a horrible husband. But I'm nothing like him, if that's what you're worried about."

"I can't do this," she said, shaking her head. "I'm not ready—" She didn't finish her thought.

"Look, I didn't expect to fall for you, either. I mean, I'm

a rancher to the core, and you're—not! But you're amazing, and I'm willing to see where this goes."

"See where it goes..." Eloise laughed bitterly. "Why, Cory? Tell me that. Because I'm not what you want. I'm not a ranching woman. I can't even ride a horse. I kill houseplants! Why on earth would you put aside what you really need?"

She had a point. So, what was he hoping—that she'd agree to be the medic and morph into a ranching woman before his eyes?

Eloise asked pointedly, "Are you hoping that I'll become someone different if I just stay here long enough?"

An image of Deirdre rose in his mind. She'd known the land, known the machines, known the livestock like no other woman in the county—he'd counted on her. When she left, Cory had resented that she'd given up on the land, but his desire to share these acres with a woman who could love them as deeply as he did hadn't waned.

"I know what I need," he admitted, scrubbing a hand through his hair. "I need a ranching woman."

"See?" Tears shone in her eyes. "I'm not going to change. I am who I am."

"And our feelings?" he pressed. "Don't they factor in at all?"

"They aren't enough," she replied with a shake of her head. "I've lived through that once already."

Eloise was right. If he couldn't accept her for who she was right now, what kind of future did they have together? But the thought of saying goodbye hurt more than he could stand.

"Would you be willing to work with me?" he asked. "Just be the medic out here. No pressure."

"No." She sucked in a breath. "I'd fall in love with you. I couldn't handle the heartbreak."

Cory nodded, his heart heavy. "Too late for me," he muttered.

Eloise brushed a tear off her cheek.

"I'm going to bed now," she said. "I just need to get my balance back. This will never work between us, Cory. So let's just keep it professional, okay?"

"Yeah," he agreed. "That's for the best."

As Eloise left the room, Cory stood alone with the floral scent of her perfume still hanging in the air.

Was he crazy to want more with a woman who was so far from what he needed around here? Probably, but his heart felt as heavy as cement inside his chest anyway. They did have their faith in common, and Eloise was a strong, resilient, trustworthy woman—all traits that he was looking for in a wife. She understood him better than anyone in this short time, but it didn't change who they were. She was city. He was country.

Eloise wasn't for him. The timing was all wrong, and at least she had the wisdom to see it.

Lord, he prayed silently, *give me the strength*...

The strength to let her go? To face reality? Cory wasn't sure. He just knew that he didn't have shoulders wide enough to carry this one on his own.

Chapter Sixteen

Cory carried the bags to his father's house on the sleepy Haggerston street. The sun was high, lighting up the day in false cheerfulness. The little bungalow crouched next to a scraggly apple tree, curtains closed and driveway empty.

The drive had been a quiet one. Cory had had so much to say, and so little at the same time. It had all been said before. Eloise was beautiful, funny, sweet—but she didn't want the life he did. What was left to discuss?

This is it. I probably won't come back here.

Eloise pushed the old man's wheelchair into the kitchen, and Cory set down their bags by the door.

"I'm tired," his father murmured.

"I'll get you settled in bed, Robert," Eloise assured him. "Let me give you your pills first, okay?"

Cory watched him as he took his medication with a few sips of water.

This is my dad. Maybe I'll look more like him when I get to his age.

He'd appreciated this opportunity to know Robert, even if the old man hadn't been what he'd expected. Meeting his dad had cleared up some questions and added a few extra, but Cory felt he understood a little more about the man who had sired him. He might not miss the old man's snarky comments, or his constant irritability, but he would miss the chance to get to know him better.

Cory hadn't known Eloise for long, either, but somehow she'd worked her way into his mind, even into his thoughts while he worked or drove. She would not be easy to forget.

Would this be his final goodbye to both of them?

His father's eyes flickered toward him.

"So this is it?" his father asked, as if reading his mind.

Cory nodded. "Looks like."

"Well, you've seen me in all my glory. What do you think?"

Cory wasn't sure what to say, and his father rasped out a laugh.

"That's what I thought," he said. "No hard feelings, boy. I take a bit to get used to."

"Thanks for coming out to the ranch," Cory said. "I wanted you to see that."

"You've done okay for yourself, kid." The old man shrugged. "I don't like long goodbyes."

His father's praise warmed him, and he nodded, trying to cover the rise of emotion. He'd waited a lifetime to hear his father say that he'd done well.

"Me, either." Cory gave the old man a grin. "I guess I get that from you."

"So, see you..." He held his son's gaze for a moment, then looked up at Eloise. "I'll go to bed now."

Eloise nodded and gave Cory a sympathetic look. "Would you wait a few minutes before you go?"

Cory nodded, and as Eloise rolled his father out of the kitchen and toward his bedroom, he let his gaze move over the room.

He noticed a tin of tea on the counter, a line of medicine bottles beside the tea. He wondered how much he could learn about his father just by looking around his kitchen.

Not a lot, he admitted to himself. *Not the things I want to know.*

The clock on the wall ticked, and from the kitchen he could hear the murmur of voices. He had no memories of the people who lived in this house, but he knew he was connected to it. His father had lived here with Ruth. He could feel the woman's touch about the place—the seventies-styled pot holders hanging on the wall, the tins lined up from smallest to largest at the top of the cupboards, fake plants collecting dust along a windowsill. Ruth could still be felt in her kitchen.

When Eloise returned, she stopped in the doorway, fatigue showing around her eyes. Pulling a hand through her curls, she brushed them away from her face.

"Thanks for waiting," she said.

"Of course." He smiled, and they sat down at the kitchen table. "I'm sorry about last night."

"No, that's okay. I guess we had to get a few things settled."

He nodded. That was true enough. "You'll tell me when he passes away, right?"

"Of course. You'll be my first call." Compassion entered her gaze and she gave him a sad smile. "How are you holding up?"

"I'm okay." He nodded. "I got to meet him, and that's more than I had before."

"So it wasn't a mistake to find you?"

"Far from it." A lump rose in his throat. "But I'm going to miss you."

Her chin trembled. "Me, too."

Cory fiddled with the rim of his hat, then dropped it onto his knee. "I'd better get going."

Eloise nodded. "I suppose."

Cory stood and went to the door, his hat in one hand. When he turned back toward her, he found her eyes focused on his, her lips parted. He longed to dip down and catch those lips in his, but he knew better.

"Come here," he said softly. When she approached he gathered her against his broad chest. She fit neatly under his arms, and he rested his cheek against her soft curls, inhaling the sweet scent of her shampoo. He held her close, feeling the patter of her heart against his shirt.

"Is this a really bad time to tell you that I'm falling in love with you?" Cory murmured.

Eloise laughed. "Yes!"

"Just checking."

She pulled back, and when she raised her eyes to meet his, he found tears sparkling. She swallowed hard.

"Take care," he said softly.

Opening the door, Cory stepped outside. Never before had walking away taken so much effort.

Chapter Seventeen

The herd was safely in the cow barn before Cory headed to the ranch house. His body ached from the work, and his arm throbbed in the damp weather. Rain fell steadily, veiling the ranch in mist, and he was wet through, despite his raincoat. A trickle of water worked its way down his spine, and when another blast of wind hit him, he shivered.

The house glowed comfortably in the distance, and he picked up his pace as wind drove into his face.

She's not there.

The realization knocked the energy out of his stride. Eloise hadn't been on his land long, but the time she was there had made an impact. He couldn't just fall back into his regular routines.

I got used to her.

It was more than that. It was deeper. He'd fallen in love with her against his better judgment.

Cory remembered the way the house used to glow when his grandparents were still alive, and he and his grandfather would trudge back home after a long day of work together.

"You know my favorite thing in the world?" his grandfather would ask.

"What?"

"The light in that window."

Cory had never fully understood his grandfather's sentiment. He'd associated it with his grandmother's delicious cooking that would be waiting for them, but now he knew different.

A light in the window meant more than a meal. It meant a person—a woman.

The wet ground squished beneath his boots, and he hunched his shoulders against the prying rain. He stomped his boots on the steps, and as he stepped inside, he shook off his raincoat and dropped his sodden hat onto a peg.

Some leftover stew remained in the fridge, and after a quick supper eaten over the kitchen sink, Cory washed the bowl, then headed to his bedroom.

Lord, I just need this day to end.

As he peeled off his work shirt, his eyes fell once more on the little metal box on his dresser. He'd taken it from the library, meaning to go through all of the letters, but had lost heart after he'd read just a few.

He stared at that box for a long moment, then picked it up and opened it. He flipped through the envelopes with the now-familiar handwriting until he came to a different envelope—the handwriting that of his mother's, not Robert's. Written across the top were the words *From Ruth Bessler.*

Cory frowned and peeled it open. Inside was a collection of bank receipts—each one for one hundred dollars. On the first of every month, a check for one hundred dollars had been cashed. He looked at the date.

"I was ten…" he murmured.

Ruth Bessler, his father's wife, had been sending money to his mother?

Suddenly the pieces clicked into place in his mind and he stood in stunned silence.

I got new clothes, new shoes, went on class trips. My

mom couldn't afford any of that. She wore the same old clothes from ten years before.

He knew exactly where those luxuries came from now. Ruth had been supporting her husband's illegitimate child all those years.

Ruth knew.

Several days passed and Eloise documented her patient's decline. He spent more time sleeping, and he grew more lethargic, less aware of things going on around him. Normally at a time like this, family members pulled close, supporting each other as they awaited the final goodbye, but Mr. Bessler faced this alone—except for his loyal nurse.

One evening, Eloise sat next to Mr. Bessler's bed, her Bible in her lap. She'd begun to spend more time sitting next to him while he slept. She wasn't sure if her presence comforted him or not. She sat next to a reading light, her Bible open to a passage in Psalms:

Are not two sparrows sold for a farthing? and one of them shall not fall on the ground without your Father. But the very hairs of your head are all numbered. Fear ye not therefore, ye are of more value than many sparrows.

Tonight this passage comforted her. Her mind went back to the vast swarms of sparrows she'd seen swooping and diving in unison at the ranch. It was miraculous that they knew how to stay together, but more amazing still that God kept track of every tiny bird in every massive swarm, and was with each one that fell.

Eloise knew she wasn't alone, but she also knew that she'd soon go back to her own "swarm" in Billings and disappear into the hubbub of the city. She would never be alone when she had God with her, but the thought still saddened her.

She missed Cory.

Her patient stirred, and she looked up from her Bible. She glanced at his medication chart to see when his next dose was due, and it was soon.

He moaned softly, his eyelids fluttering open, then shut again.

"Red?" he murmured.

"I'm here, Robert."

"I'm cold."

Eloise grabbed another blanket and settled it over him, but he didn't seem satisfied. He licked his lips and his eyes fluttered open again.

"Are you in pain?" she asked softly. "I could give you your next dose now, if you need it."

"It hurts," he whispered. "But no."

"Are you sure?"

"I don't want to sleep…" His voice trailed away.

"What do you need?"

"Where's Cory?"

Eloise wondered if he'd lost track of time. "You're at home, Robert. Cory went back to his ranch."

The old man nodded slowly. "I forgot."

"It's okay," she reassured him. "Everything is fine."

"I'm not ready to die," he said, and Eloise felt tears rise in her eyes.

"I'm not a bad man, Red."

"I know that."

"I only found God a few years ago. My wife—" He swallowed and licked at his dry lips. "My wife prayed for years that I'd find Jesus."

"And you did," she whispered, bringing a cup of water to his lips. He took a sip.

"Not soon enough." He shook his head, a tear trickling down his lined cheek. "I ruined too many lives before I changed."

"Did Ruth know that you found God?" she asked softly.

"We had ten good years together, but I don't think they were enough to make up for the other forty."

"Robert," she said firmly, "that isn't for you to judge. Leave that to God, okay?"

"It would have been different," he whispered. "If I'd let God change me earlier, my whole life would have been better. I would have been good to her..."

"She's safe with God. She's not in pain, and she's not angry. You'll see her soon."

"I know." He swallowed with some difficulty. His words broke off, and he gestured feebly toward the Bible in her hands. "Read to me."

Eloise picked up her Bible and opened it to the twenty-third Psalm.

"'The Lord is my shepherd, I shall not be in want...'"

The words were familiar and comforting. Mr. Bessler's breath came more shallowly. She glanced up several times as she read through some of her own favorite Bible passages, and the last time she raised her eyes, Mr. Bessler's chest was still, his face ashen, his mouth limp.

The old man had died.

"It's over," she murmured past the lump in her throat. She reached for the old man's frail hand and took it in hers.

She hadn't expected to cry. The tears welled up inside her until she couldn't hold them back anymore. They spilled down her cheeks, silently at first, and then past her careful control until she wept openly into her hands.

Eloise cried for the heartbreak of a life lived with regrets, for the sorrow of a child whose father didn't want him, for marriages that went sour, for husbands who walked out and for fathers who walked away.

Eloise cried for Philip, who hadn't given them a chance, for the baby she'd longed for but never conceived, for the life of love and marriage that she'd worked so hard toward but had watched disintegrate.

But more than that, she wept for her friend Robert Bessler, a difficult old man who'd made his share of mistakes and had wrestled with them for a lifetime. Despite his shortcomings, he'd been a more honest friend than some people in her life.

When her tears were spent, the sun was just peeking above the horizon, scarlet light seeping into the room through the crack in the curtains.

"Rest in peace, Robert," Eloise whispered.

Chapter Eighteen

The next day Eloise went home and slept for longer than she'd slept in months. She didn't awake until nearly noon, and when she got out of her familiar bed in her own apartment, she sucked in a deep breath.

Another job was complete. She would put her name on the roster for a new position when she felt rested enough take on the work. Until then, she had some time to herself.

Eloise stepped into the bright kitchen and looked out the window over the park. Though her freezer was stocked and her cupboards always had a good stash of nonperishable items for times like these, she wasn't hungry. She bypassed the food and went straight to her easel, standing up in the brightest corner of the kitchen.

I need to paint.

With brushes and tubes of acrylics waiting for her touch, she stood before the easel, her mind whirring.

Some thoughts were too deep for words. Some things she didn't even know how to lift up to God in prayer, so she lifted them up in the only way she knew how— through her art.

Opening a tube of paint, Eloise squirted a dollop of yellow onto a paint board, a dab of red, some white.

Lord, hear my prayer...

* * *

Eloise parked her car in front the old house and looked at it with a pang of sadness. It had been two weeks since Mr. Bessler died, and just as long since she'd been in Haggerston. There hadn't been a funeral, since Mr. Bessler had stipulated against one in his will. The windows gaped curtainless, and a steady flow of professional movers strode in and out of the front door, boxes in hand. A moving truck waited in the drive and she sat in her car for a moment, observing the scene.

Cory stepped out the front door, his gaze moving over the street and stopping at Eloise's car. A grin spread over his rugged features and he angled his steps in her direction as she got out.

"Hi," he said with a grin as she slammed the door shut. "You're a sight for sore eyes."

He wrapped his arms around her and gave her a squeeze. Eloise shut her eyes for a moment, enjoying the scent of him. Stepping back, he caught her hand in his and led the way toward the house.

"Thanks for coming," he said.

"You knew I would," she replied with a smile. "What's happening?"

"They're moving my dad's things out. You gave my number to the pastor of his church, and he gave me a call and asked if there was anything I wanted to remember my father by. I asked for his and Ruth's wedding rings."

Eloise looked up in surprise. "Why?"

"Since scattering Ruth's ashes went so wrong, I wanted to bury their wedding rings in that spot—to make it up to my father, somehow, I suppose."

"That's sweet." She smiled. "I have a feeling Robert would have approved."

As they crossed the lawn and walked up the steps and in the front door, she looked around. Bare walls were coated in fresh white paint. The footsteps of the movers echoed through the small house.

"It feels so different in here," she said.

Cory nodded. "I know."

Cory looked down at her hand still in his and ran a thumb over her fingers. "You've been painting this morning."

She smiled and nodded. "I've finally painted a full portrait."

"Head to toe?" he asked in surprise.

"Head to toe." Eloise chuckled. "I was ready for it."

"Who did you paint?" he asked. "Your mom? Your dad?"

"No, a self-portrait."

Her mind went back to the canvas in the middle of her kitchen. It was a large piece, depicting herself standing with hands on hips, eyes directed toward the viewer. It hadn't been easy to pull the pieces all together, but if she was going to capture an entire person, the layers and subtleties combined, who better to start with than the woman she knew best? It had taken nearly two weeks, and three new starts before she got it right. Eloise may have balked at capturing all of a person, but she now believed in embracing all of herself. In painting it, her heart raised in prayer, she'd also untangled a few knots in regard to her marriage. When she last looked at it, she'd felt a swell of satisfaction.

That's me.

"Look," Cory said, turning her to face him. "I've discovered a few things."

"Like what?" She met his gaze, frowning slightly.

"In that stack of letters we found in the library, there was another envelope my mother tucked in there. It was full of bank receipts. My mother got monthly checks from Ruth."

Eloise blinked. "I don't get it. I didn't think Ruth knew about you."

"She must have, because she sent money regularly to help my mother out."

Eloise shook her head. "She was willing to help her husband's child from another woman?"

Cory and Eloise stepped back as two movers came by with a chest of drawers. Cory nodded toward Mr. Bessler's empty bedroom and they moved in there for privacy. It echoed with their footsteps, awash in sunlight.

"This is part of why I wanted to do something for her—a thank-you of sorts."

They stood in silence for several moments, the footsteps of movers echoing through the house. Finally, Cory cleared his throat.

"You asked me before if you were the kind of woman I needed, and I said no."

Eloise nodded, the memory still painful. "It's okay. It was the truth."

"Yeah, well, I've had some time to think on that." Cory dropped his gaze and hooked a thumb into a belt loop. "I thought I needed a certain kind of woman—a country girl who could rope a steer. The thing is, my dad had the right kind of woman, even if he didn't treat her right. He had a woman who loved God, and her faith made her into a better lady than any of us ever realized. And that's what I want—a woman with heart. A woman connected to God." He raised his dark eyes to meet hers. "You."

Eloise felt her cheeks heat at his gentle scrutiny. A smile flickered at the corners of his lips. He pulled off his hat and tossed it onto the windowsill.

"I miss you," he said.

She nodded. "Me, too."

"The question is, can you trust me?" He reached up and moved a curl away from her temple.

Her gaze wandered around the empty room. "I always felt that I could trust you, Cory. I just couldn't trust my own judgment."

"And now?"

"Philip was a fraud, but I wanted to believe in him more than I wanted to see the facts. That's where I went wrong—I was so concerned with the role of wife that I forgot to be me first."

"If my vote counts, I like you the way you are," Cory said.

She laughed softly. "Thanks. So do I."

"Whatever happened between Robert and Ruth—" Cory began.

"He found God too late," Eloise interjected. "Or at least that's what he thought. Most of their marriage, he wasn't a believer." She paused, remembering her patient's last hours. "But they're both with God now."

"And we're here." Cory caught her gaze and held it, as if he longed for her to understand something deeper in his words.

"We're here." Eloise nodded, swallowing hard. "Cory, I was so wrong. I let you walk away, and when I had time to think, all I could think about was you. I—"

The words caught in her throat.

"I love you," he said softly.

"I love you, too, Cory." The words came out in a breathy rush. She was relieved to finally say them.

"Then what are we waiting for?" He stepped closer and slid his strong hand down her arm. "I want to marry you."

Eloise stood speechless for a long moment. She swallowed and looked away but felt her eyes drawn back to his ruggedly handsome face.

"I'm still not a rancher," she confessed. "I obviously

can't ride, I've grown up in a city and I've told you what I do to houseplants."

"I don't care about any of that," Cory replied with a shake of his head. "I'm in love with you. I love your depth and your sweetness, the fact that you paint your feelings out, the way you think, the way you move… I love you, Eloise. So you can be a downright terrible rancher. I don't need you to fill a role for me, just be faithful. I need you by my side. And there is one thing I can promise—no matter what life throws at us, I'll be the best husband to you I possibly can."

Tears welled in her eyes. "You say that now…but what about later?"

"What about later?" he asked softly.

"Will you change your mind?"

"Eloise, you've had me from hello," he murmured, running a finger down her cheek.

Her breath caught in her throat as he moved closer still, slipping his arms around her waist.

Eloise searched his eyes, looking for guile. Instead she saw the beginnings of a smile. He dipped his head, catching her lips in his. She sank into his embrace, his strong arms pressing her close against his heartbeat.

When he pulled away, her knees felt wobbly. "I just hope you aren't too attached to your houseplants, Cory."

"Is that a yes?" he whispered.

"Yes!" Eloise nodded, her eyes misting with unshed tears.

As he pulled her back into a kiss, Eloise felt safer than she had in a long time. She wouldn't be able to describe the moment, the way her heart had soared, the fragility of her hope enveloped in the strength of his love. It would be a memory that left her blissfully speechless. A few years later, she would paint it—a couple silhouetted against a sunlit window, a cowboy hat balanced on the windowsill.

She would call it *Coming Home*.

It would be her deepest prayer of thanksgiving.

Epilogue

Cory dropped another pile of lumber at the base of a mature oak tree and looked up into the branches. The leafy canopy glowed green as the late-morning sunlight filtered through. He could already see the finished product in his mind's eye—a stable floor and tall walls with windows cut into the sides. A rope ladder would hang down from the front door, brushing the grass and swinging in the wind. He hadn't decided on the roof yet, whether it should be sloped or flat.

Cory turned back toward his truck for another load of wood and paused when he saw his wife strolling up to where he stood. Her hair hung down, loose and tangled from the wind. A cream sundress rippled around her growing figure, and when the wind blew against her, her pregnant form brought a slow smile to his face. They'd been married for two years now, and it still felt like yesterday that he'd said "I do."

"What are you doing?" Eloise asked, lifting her lips for a kiss.

Cory kissed her and ran his hand over her silky curls. "Getting ready for the baby."

She laughed, her gaze moving to the pile of wood at the base of the tree. "How, exactly?"

"You can't see it?" Cory pulled her in front of him and slid his arms around her. "Do you see that bough there?"

He pointed toward the biggest limb.

"Mmm-hmm." Her voice was low and sweet, like brown sugar.

"If you follow it back, there's another bough at the same height. That's going to hold up the floor of the tree house. I want the walls to be high enough that I can get inside there, too. I'll have windows on two sides, and the third side is going to be against the trunk. Do you see?"

"A tree house?" She shifted to look back at him. "But the baby can't use a tree house, Cory."

"Maybe not right away, but little girls grow fast, you know."

"You still think this baby is a girl?" Eloise grinned.

"With ginger curls like her mother's."

"And what if we have a boy?" she asked with a chuckle.

"Then I won't do a shingled roof. I'll make it into a ship, complete with mast and a sail." Cory turned his attention back to the tree, the tree house coming together in his mind as he imagined the sunny, summer days that would be whiled away.

"I came to tell you that lunch is ready," she said.

Cory pulled his thoughts out of the tree limbs and gave her a slow smile. "Are we on our own for the afternoon?"

"No." Eloise laughed and gave him a swat. "My dad is waiting for us. You know that. Three more days, and then you and I are alone again." The sparkle in her eye held promise. "Oh, he said that he wants to go riding with you this afternoon, if you're not too busy."

"I'll take him with me to check on the herd."

"This is such a vacation for him. He loves all this ranch stuff, you know."

Cory took her hand and moved the pad of his thumb over the paint-stained cuticles on her slender fingers. He'd take her father riding, and she'd likely pour herself into another painting for her art show in the fall.

"What did you paint today?" he asked.

"Something I've been trying to put into words lately..."

"How ruggedly handsome your husband is?" he teased.

Eloise laughed and rolled her eyes. "No, how I felt when you asked me to marry you."

"And how did you feel?"

"You'll have to see it. Then you'll know." She shot him a grin. "Come on. Lunch will get cold if you don't hurry up."

Eloise pulled ahead of him, stepping high over the grass as she made her way to the waiting pickup. She moved more cautiously as her body grew with her pregnancy; she walked with the belabored grace of impending motherhood.

She's beautiful... He'd never felt more love or contentedness than when he looked at Eloise and remembered that she was his—Mrs. Eloise Stone.

Cory stole one last look at the towering oak, and he jogged to catch up. He was a simple man, but he gave what he could: a heart filled with devotion to his gorgeous wife, and a tree house, built too early, for the baby he couldn't wait to meet.

* * * * *

Dear Reader,

I'm a city girl. Well, at least I was. I lived in Toronto, Canada, for many years, and I loved the city life—everything from the shopping to the restaurants. I enjoyed walking everywhere I went, or just hopping on a bus. There is something quite exhilarating about a city—the thrum of energy, the ebb and flow of people, and the ability to melt into a crowd.

Then I got married and we moved out to a small town. It's small enough that every time I go out, I see someone I recognize. It's not really possible to melt into crowds here, and I'm enjoying that. Everyone at church knows my little boy's name. I can smile and wave at people I recognize driving past. It's a whole new world, but a comfortable one. The thrum of energy has been replaced by the warmth of community, and I'm truly happy.

Change is never graceful, though, is it? At least not for me. I still have three locks on my front door. I lock people *in* when they visit me, because an unlocked front door just seems risky to my city-girl mentality. I still zone out when I grocery-shop so people have to actually ram their shopping carts into me to get my attention. Our "Stranger Danger" rules are probably a lot more excessive than everyone else's. Yet here we are, and we are most certainly Home. For me, Home is in my husband's arms.

You see, Home is about being exactly who you are—clumsy tendencies, horrible singing voice and a ridiculous number of locks on your door—and still belonging. Home might be about crayon-colored Mother's Day cards, or about the man who pulls you close and tells you that you're gorgeous. It might be about the group of girlfriends who pull you out of your funk, or about the church family that rallies around you and gives you the courage to face another week. Home is about the people who truly know you and say, "You're one of us."

We've been taught to wait for the right man or for the right circumstances to declare ourselves Home, but I have a different idea: if you aren't Home yet, stop waiting. Let's make Home right here. Right now. Let's love the ones God puts in our paths, enjoy the blessings pouring down and embrace the person God created us to be. I can guarantee you this: you are the answer to someone's deepest prayer.

Come find me on Facebook at Patricia Johns Romance, or come by my blog at PatriciaJohnsRomance.com. If you message me, I'll answer. You have my word on that.

Chin up, ladies. We're in this together...and together is the best way to be.

Patricia

Questions for Discussion

1. Eloise struggles with trust after her husband leaves her for another woman. What people or events in your life have affected your sense of self-worth?

2. Cory always wondered about his biological father when he was growing up, but he wasn't ready to find out the truth about his parents. In his position, would you rather know the worst, or keep your innocence? Why?

3. Mr. Bessler is a good friend to Eloise but a terrible father to Cory. Do you think it's possible to excel in one role and fail in another and still be a good person?

4. Cory says that his land is something that reminds him of who he is. What fills that role for you—anchors you against the storms of life?

5. Mr. Bessler claims that his past mistakes are private and no one else's business. Do you agree with him, or do you think that when our mistakes affect others, they have a right to address them?

6. Cory discovers that Ruth did know about the affair after all but chose not only to stay in the marriage, but to support Cory financially while he was growing up. Do you think Ruth made the right decision, or was she being a "doormat"?

7. Eloise believes that she put too much of herself into her first marriage, and not enough into her own inter-

ests. How important do you think it is for a woman to maintain her individuality in marriage?

8. Eloise wants to know the secret to a happy, lasting marriage. What advice would you give her?

REQUEST YOUR FREE BOOKS!

2 FREE INSPIRATIONAL NOVELS

PLUS 2
FREE
MYSTERY GIFTS

Love Inspired

YES! Please send me 2 FREE Love Inspired® novels and my 2 FREE mystery gifts (gifts are worth about $10). After receiving them, if I don't wish to receive any more books, I can return the shipping statement marked "cancel." If I don't cancel, I will receive 6 brand-new novels every month and be billed just $4.74 per book in the U.S. or $5.24 per book in Canada. That's a saving of at least 21% off the cover price. It's quite a bargain! Shipping and handling is just 50¢ per book in the U.S. and 75¢ per book in Canada.* I understand that accepting the 2 free books and gifts places me under no obligation to buy anything. I can always return a shipment and cancel at any time. Even if I never buy another book, the two free books and gifts are mine to keep forever.   105/305 IDN F47Y

Name	(PLEASE PRINT)	
Address		Apt. #
City	State/Prov.	Zip/Postal Code

Signature (if under 18, a parent or guardian must sign)

Mail to the **Harlequin®** Reader Service:
IN U.S.A.: P.O. Box 1867, Buffalo, NY 14240-1867
IN CANADA: P.O. Box 609, Fort Erie, Ontario L2A 5X3

**Are you a subscriber to Love Inspired books
and want to receive the larger-print edition?
Call 1-800-873-8635 or visit www.ReaderService.com.**

* Terms and prices subject to change without notice. Prices do not include applicable taxes. Sales tax applicable in N.Y. Canadian residents will be charged applicable taxes. Offer not valid in Quebec. This offer is limited to one order per household. Not valid for current subscribers to Love Inspired books. All orders subject to credit approval. Credit or debit balances in a customer's account(s) may be offset by any other outstanding balance owed by or to the customer. Please allow 4 to 6 weeks for delivery. Offer available while quantities last.

Your Privacy—The Harlequin® Reader Service is committed to protecting your privacy. Our Privacy Policy is available online at www.ReaderService.com or upon request from the Harlequin Reader Service.

We make a portion of our mailing list available to reputable third parties that offer products we believe may interest you. If you prefer that we not exchange your name with third parties, or if you wish to clarify or modify your communication preferences, please visit us at www.ReaderService.com/consumerchoice or write to us at Harlequin Reader Service Preference Service, P.O. Box 9062, Buffalo, NY 14269. Include your complete name and address.

LI13R

"Are you hurt?"

Dorcas froze. She didn't recognize this stranger's voice.
Frantically, she attempted to cover her bare shins. "I'm
caught," she squeaked out. "My dress…"

"*Ne, maedle*, lie still."

She squinted at him in the sunshine. This was no lad,
but a young man. She clamped her eyes shut, hoping the
ground would swallow her up.

She felt the tension on her dress suddenly loosen.

"There you go."

Before she could protest, he was lifting her out of the
briars.

He cradled her against him. "Best I get you to Sara and
have her take a look at that knee. Might need stitches." He
started to walk across the field toward Sara's.

Dorcas looked into a broad, shaven face framed by
shaggy butter-blond hair that hung almost to his wide
shoulders. He was the most attractive man she had ever
laid eyes on. He was too beautiful to be real, this man
with merry pewter-gray eyes and suntanned skin.

*I must have hit the post with my head and knocked
myself silly*, she thought.

"I can…" She pushed against his shoulders, thinking she should walk.

"*Ne*, you could do yourself more harm." He shifted her weight. "You'll be more comfortable if you put your arms around my neck."

"I…I…" she mumbled, but she did as he said. She knew that this was improper, but she couldn't figure out what to do.

"You must be the little cousin Sara said was coming to help her today," he said. "I'm Gideon Esch, her hired man. From Wisconsin."

Little? She was five foot eleven, a giant compared to most of the local women. No one had ever called her *little* before.

"You don't say much, do you?" He looked down at her in his arms and grinned.

Dorcas nodded.

He grinned. "I like you. Do you have a name?"

"Dorcas. Dorcas Coblentz."

"You don't look like a Dorcas to me."

He stopped walking to look down at her. "I don't suppose you have a middle name?"

"Adelaide."

"Adelaide," he repeated. "Addy. You look a lot more like an Addy than you do a Dorcas."

"Addy?" The idea settled over her as easily as warm maple syrup over blueberry pancakes. "Addy," she repeated, and then she found herself smiling back at him.

Will Addy fall for the handsome Amish handyman?
Pick up A MATCH FOR ADDY to find out!
Available February 2015,
wherever Love Inspired® books and ebooks are sold.

"What's wrong, Ella?" Josiah's dark blue eyes filled with concern.

Words stuck in her throat. She fought the tears welling in her. "My son is missing," she finally squeaked out.

"Where? When?" he asked, suddenly all business.

"About an hour ago at Camp Yukon. I hope you can help look for him."

"Let's go. My truck is outside." Josiah fell into step next to her.

Ella slid a glance toward him, and the sight of Josiah, a former US marine, calmed her nerves. She knew how good he was with his dog at finding people. Robbie would be all right. She had to believe that. The alternative was unthinkable.

He opened the back door for his dog, Buddy, then quickly moved to the front door for Ella. "I'll find Robbie. I promise."

The confidence in his voice further eased her anxiety. Ella climbed into the cab with Josiah's hand on her elbow.

As he started the engine, Ella ran her hands up and down her arms. But the chill burrowed its way into the marrow of her bones, even though the temperature was sixty-five.

Josiah glanced at her. "David will get plenty of people to scour the whole park. Do you have anything with Robbie's scent on it?"

"I do. In my car."

He backed up to her black Jeep Wrangler. "Where?"

"Front seat. A jacket he didn't take with him."

Josiah jumped out of the truck to get it before Ella had a chance to even open her door.

He returned quickly with Robbie's brown jacket in his grasp.

He gave it to Ella. "This will help Buddy find your son."

Ella leaned forward, staring out the windshield at the sky. Dark clouds drifted over the sun. "Looks like we'll have a storm late this afternoon."

Josiah's strong jawline twitched. "We can still search in the rain, but let's hope that the weatherman is wrong."

Ella closed her eyes. She had to remain calm and in control. That was one of the things she'd always been able to do in the middle of a search and rescue, but this time it was her son.

"Ella, I promise you," Josiah said. "I won't leave the park until we find your son."

Will Robbie be found before nightfall?
Pick up TO SAVE HER CHILD to find out.
Available February 2015, wherever
Love Inspired® Suspense books and ebooks are sold.

JUST CAN'T GET ENOUGH OF INSPIRATIONAL ROMANCE?

Join our social communities
and talk to us online!
You will have access to the latest
news on upcoming titles and special
promotions, but most important,
you can talk to other fans about your
favorite Love Inspired® reads.

 www.Facebook.com/LoveInspiredBooks

 www.Twitter.com/LoveInspiredBks

Harlequin.com/Community

LISOCIAL